WHEN THE CLOCK STRIKES 2.a.m.

Joe Somerville

To my lovely wife Sylvia, Candy &
Rocky
Dedicated to our wonderful son Dale

God needed another angel in heaven so
he chose our son Dale to be one of the
best

By the same author of
The Purple Rose

Detective Chief Inspector Jack Farley stubbed out his fourth cigarette in an ash tray and prepared to go home to his self-contained flat in Swiss Cottage.

He missed the companionship of his former partner Nick Stone, and somehow his office in New Scotland Yard did not seem the same without him.

Although Nick's promotion board had been long overdue, he missed the laughs and jokes they had together, and he had passed the inspector's exam with flying colours.

In two months' time Nick would be getting married to his lovely fiancée Candy Crystal, and Jack will be giving her away.

Also coming from America will be Don Grant the F.B.I. agent they met in Miami, and Jack looked forward to meeting him again.

Jack's new replacement for Nick was Sergeant Roger Osborn, who was drafted

in from Berkhamsted, a town in rural
Hertfordshire three months earlier, having
asked to be transferred to the
Metropolitan Police to better himself for
promotion and taking care of his wife
Elsie and young family,a five year old
boy Gary, and a seven year old girl,
Vicky.
Jack was his own man and saw things in
black and white, if a person or persons
committed a serious crime they deserved
more punishment than the courts gave,
and he got steamed up when a grinning
criminal got off with just a community
order that was rarely finished.
Roger on the other hand, done everything
by the book, and even after three months
still called Jack sir.
He rarely argued and would not commit
himself until he was absolutely sure of
the facts.
It was just after 2 a.m. and as Jack put his
coat on to go home his phone rang.
He thought twice about answering it,
almost tasting the fish and chip supper
he had promised himself at the all night

cafe on the way home.

But picking up the phone he said."Farley here, what's that? a woman's been murdered, where? o.k. I'm on my way, get sergeant Osborn to meet me at Parliament square as soon as possible."

Sergeant Roger Osborn was already there taking down notes of what P. C. Newton had seen at 2 a.m. precisely, as Big Ben struck the hour.

"I was about a hundred yards away, and in the dim light I saw the figures of a man and a woman standing together, then the woman gave a piercing scream and fell to the ground and the man ran off,

I gave chase but was too far away to get any description of him, and I stopped at the woman's body to check her pulse, but her throat had been slit open from ear to ear and I immediately called in for assistance."

Looking at him, the sergeant thought, "The size of you mate, you could waddle faster than you could run," but said instead, "Thank you constable, D.C.I. Farley will speak to you later."

After taping off the area and leaving two men to patrol the square, they started back to the response car when another call came through that a second woman had been savagely murdered with her throat cut in Trafalgar Square.

A night cleaner on his way home had seen her sprawled on the pavement, at first he thought it was a bag lady sleeping rough, but stepping round her saw the fresh blood in the light of his torch and immediately dialled 999 on his mobile.

"We are on our way," replied Jack Farley, "Over and out."

Do you think these two murders maybe connected sir?" asked Roger, "I reckon It's too coincidental not to be." he added.

"I'd be surprised if it's not mate," replied Jack. "And a pound to a pinch of shit it's the same person responsible, since you've been here it's been normal police work, and you've been let off lightly so far, now we've been brought in it means there could be big problems, you will find it's a lot different to the odd break in or fight in

Berkhamsted, so don't be conned by flowery words or lame excuses, just be friendly but firm, and trust no one until you are sure of the facts, sometimes you've got to throw the rule book away and fight fire with fire, if you get my meaning, and for god's sake stop calling me sir, I've not been knighted yet, call me guv, or Jack, like Nick Stone did, you got that.? "

"Yes sir, er, guv. I will try to from now on; at my interview the commissioner told me you were very unconventional and although you are a great policeman and good at your job, not to copy your ways too much if I wanted to be noticed for all the right reasons.

Sorry about that but I thought you should know."

Jack just laughed and said. "No sweat mate, me and the top brass just put up with each other; they turn a blind eye to my methods when it suits them, and sometimes call me in for a bollocking when the shit hits the fan!"

Arriving at Trafalgar Square they made their way to the doorway where the woman's body still lay, the police photographer had just finished his task and the ambulance was about to take the body away for examination.

Even at that hour there were a number of people around, as although the street lighting cast many shadows, the two detectives hoped that someone had witnessed what had happened.

Jack looked around at the seven or eight onlookers and said. "Did anyone here see what happened? don't give me any old crap, just yes or no!"

Some were talking among themselves. Then an Irishman who was a little worse for wear came nearer to Jack and said. "My name is Declan Flanagan so it is, an' That's Molly Ryan, I only left her about ten minutes ago, she's a lovely woman, we both came from Dublin an' I've known her for years the little darlin', she's on the game I know, but she always gave me a handout fiver for a couple of jars like she did tonight, an' as I walked away I turned to wave to her but It seemed a punter was waiting for me to go, he was sideways to me when I turned so I moved away, if I'd have known he was gonna kill my little friend begorrah, I'd 'ave topped the bastard myself so I would."

"I'm sure you would have," said jack, "I know our Molly, she has been around the block a few years now, and didn't deserve that. Did you get a good look at him?" asked Jack hopefully.

"No sir," he replied, "I never saw his face 'cos he was sideways to me, but the bloke was a big 'un, well over six foot an' he had no 'at on, with lightish wavy hair, that's all I can tell you sir, begorrah now, there was one thing more sir, I'll be sure to be thinkin,' he may 'ave 'ad a slight limp so he did, anyway you can nearly always find me round 'Paddy's bar,' he pays me for doing odd jobs for himself now and then so he does."

"That description could fit half the men in London, apart from a maybe limp," thought Jack, "But it's a start anyway."

Jack thanked him and slipped him a five-pound note as he walked away.

Roger Osborn was taking notes from three people, but mainly they were not very helpful. Each one giving a different description of what they thought they had seen and heard.

One thought he was coloured, another said he had a distinct limp, and the third said he saw his face for a moment and thought he had a moustache.

He took their details and told them they may be contacted again.

"Nothing more we can do till the morning," said Jack, "I know an all-night fish and chip bar near here, join me and I will fill you in about Molly Ryan, and Ron Ravenhill, yes mate that one, before he became one of the big time villains that is now a household name, he met her while on holiday in Ireland, he was a charmer with the ladies and promised her the good life if she came with him to London, well mate, the kid was a bit naïve, and never having been out of Ireland she jumped at the chance,

but once over here he put her in the care of his sister Lola, who likes to be called Lucrecia, just like the villain of old.
She is as wicked as they come.
Ravenhill, or "The Colonel" as he is known by, was court marshalled and thrown out of the army for breaking the jaw of a colonel and was put in the army nick at Colchester for six months, but he scared seven sort of shit out of the guards there, they couldn't get rid of him quick enough, that's the kind of man he is, some call him the smiling assassin as he grins a lot and doesn't take prisoners."
"Another cuppa mate?" he asked his sergeant.
Then continued, "Lucrecia is still a good looking woman, but her eyes are as hard as nails, she has a school of around fifty prostitutes that rake in thousands a week, not much we can about that, except pull a couple of their tarts in now and then, and they get fined a few quid, then poor Molly was forced to join them and made to live on a pittance, being threatened with a branding iron and being

kneecapped if she ever tried to leave their set up, she was made to write home to her parents every now and then saying how much she loved London, about three months ago the Ravenhill's told her she was free to go her own way, but warned her to stay shtum, tell no one, and stay off their manor, now the poor kid has been murdered and for what reason though ? she was harmless and didn't get any of life's breaks, if I find the killer first I'll ..."

Roger Osborn looked as his chief and said. "Don't tell me what you'll do sir, I mean guv. I can see what the commissioner meant about you, being unconventional,what I don't see you do, or hear you say, if under oath I could not say anything untoward, I want to work alongside you, but I must play by the rules."

Jack laughed out loud saying, "I just hope you don't get too disillusioned mate, in London its dog eat dog in Berkhamsted they roll up the pavements at night, but London is a city that doesn't sleep."

Back at Scotland Yard after making out their reports Jack said. "What are your thoughts of the Met. Police now Roger, is seeing the other side of London putting you off? and how has it affected you wife and children having to move much nearer to the city? It's disrupted your home life, friends and neighbour wise quite a lot I would think? "

"Yes and no," he replied, "Elsie my wife does miss her friends, but backs me up all the way, and knows all I am doing is for all of us as a family, the children are still excited now they can see the London eye and Tower Bridge, I do expect to see more bloodshed and violence in the Met. so to your answer guv. I am not put off, and want to catch whoever done these murders as much as you do,and hopefully we will."

Jack looked at him and said."Trust me on that one mate, we will."

On the other side of The River Thames stood a mansion house with a large garden that had huge iron gates and a sentry hut with communication and video access to the house that always had someone on duty, and was patrolled by Doberman guard dogs.

The notorious Hooper twin brothers who ran their own "empire," and was known to have friends in high places owned it, and it was common knowledge that some politicians were somehow involved in their business transactions.

Both of the Hooper's were big men; Bert was around 6 ft 6 ins. tall and had a slight limp from his cage fighting days. Bill was a little shorter, but around eighteen stone of solid bone and muscle and had a very short and violent temper, only his own kind, or the very silly would argue with him.

They had a strict protection and enforcement racket in many clubs and strip joints in the west end that they did not own themselves, but got well paid for their services that were sometimes needed.

Although anyone not paying the going rate to be 'looked after,' or refusing to pay, either had their club torched or a visit from Bill Hooper or both, and nobody made the mistake of not paying again or going to the police.

None of the villains cared or bothered about the news that the old gang boss Solomon Jacobs had been killed in Miami.

He was one long established gang leader now out of the way and who ever tried to muscle in and take over his old manor would have a fight on their hands.

And it was commom knowledge the Hooper twins feared no man alive.

The Daily newspapers soon had the lurid story of the double killings.

 leaving nothing to the imagination with headlines stating. "A New Jack The Ripper Stalks London."

Also "Terror, As Two women Have Their Throats Slashed near Big Ben at 2. a.m. and so far the police have nothing to go on."

Jack's boss called them both into his office and said straight away.

"Find this nutter and nail him as soon as you can Jack, you'll get all the help I can give you, and there are others out there doing what they can, but this is more in your line, I'll look the other way as much as I can so use your own methods, just don't get caught doing them!"

He looked straight at Roger Osborn and said. "You never heard me say that, just follow Jack's lead, if he hadn't been a policeman he would have made a master criminal! now get out both of you and find something that will help calm the public."

Bill Hooper looked at his Brother Bert and said. "What do you make of that tart being slashed in Trafalgar Square Bert? do you think it's a one off or maybe someone's trying to muscle in on our patch, 'cos no outsiders gonna live if that's the case."

Bert took a long drag on his expensive Havana cigar and looked at his brother before saying, "No way bruv. the way I see it is someone's got it in for all hookers, there's one tart topped on Ravenhill's manor as well as ours, and he won't let it go, so maybe someone's got a

dose of syph. or somethin' off one of 'em an' don't like a blobby knob, just make sure the boys keep a close eye on our crumpet, 'cos although they aint any of our tarts topped yet, one of 'em might be next, an' we don't take that lyin' down!"
Jack had a message left on his answer phone from an old friend who had been blind since he was about five years old, but he could tell different people by their footstep's, his informant said he might well have some information that could prove useful, but to phone him first.
Back at his office he phoned blind Ted who told him he was just going out, but would be would be back in his flat in a couple of hours as he has a bit of business to do first, and he was sure he could help the two detectives.
Jack knew he liked the betting shops for the horses and smiled at Roger saying.
"This could be the break we are looking for mate, blind Ted has an amazing memory, if he heard the way you walk a few times, he would know who it was and pick you out as if he had seen you, I've

known him for years, and trust whatever he tells me is pukka gen, he is a real diamond of a man, you will like him mate."

"Great stuff sir, I mean guv. anyone that you know for whatever reason, I will make a note of, I can now see why our boss lets you do things your own way and turns a blind eye to it most times, so I'm lucky to be your sergeant." "Bullshit."! Said Jack and they both laughed out loud. Meanwhile blind Ted was humming a tune to himself, pleased that he had won a few pounds on the horses and had a couple of pints in the Red Lion pub with some friends before saying ta-ta and making his way home.

Sometimes he wished he lived on the ground floor and not the third, as the lift was nearly always out of order, but it was safer higher up as it was not the best of estate tower blocks to live in, and he was very independent and popular with his neighbours and had lived in that area all his life.

Making his way up the flights of steps he

stopped halfway to enjoy a mouthful of whisky from his hip flask as he always did, then continue to the third floor. Passing a neighbour who was going down he said, "Hello Sid, I can tell you've bought a new pair of shoes."

"Dead right Ted mate," came the reply, "I bet you even know that they are size nines!"

His flat was some thirty yards away when he suddenly stopped on hearing footsteps coming towards him.

He tilted his head to one side and gave a half smile before saying. "Hello mate, what brings you to this neck of the woods?"

"You did Ted!" came the reply, "I passed by you near one of the lions at Nelson's column the other night in Trafalgar Square shortly after 2.a.m. and wondered if you sussed it was me, I thought not at the time, but you shouldn't have been out that late it's bad for your health."

He gave a mirthless laugh, and carried on talking, "If you hadn't answered that copper Farley's call I wouldn't have known, but that tart had to die and your next, so it's over the balcony for you now people will think you was pissed and fell over, and I'll tell you what mate, I will take flowers to your funeral!"

Ted felt his arm being pushed up painfully behind his back as he was forced over the edge of the balcony.

"Help me somebody, anybody, help, he's trying to kill me," screamed Ted, "Farley the copper and his mate are on their way here now, help me, help me please!"

Ted was a frail man, and although he tried to struggle free, he stood no chance to escape and was thrown over the edge by his laughing assailant just as the two detectives arrived in the square.

Jack Farley jumped out of the car even before it had stopped and raced over to the crumpled form as it hit the ground.

"Good grief, its blind Ted," he spoke out loud to an empty square.

"Ted old friend, can you hear me?"

He asked, as he felt for a pulse, and saw the blood seep from his open mouth, then called out to Roger Osborn to get an ambulance immediately.

Sadly, he could see the fall had killed his old friend, and although he had seen death many times in different ways,
he had a lump in his throat and a tear in his eye for the loss of someone he cared for.

The area was taped off and the forensic team were examining the third floor and walkway for any possible clues as to what had happened.

Roger looked at his chief and said.

"For what it's worth guv doesn't blame yourself, poor old Ted had his set ways from what you have told me, and what he was going to tell you would have been in his own good time, we know he didn't fall over, let's sort this one for blind Ted."

Jack nodded his head and said. "To bloody true we will mate, then you'll see the nasty side of me, and from now on I take this as very personal!"

Chapter 2

Ron Ravenhill and his sister were going over what had happened to Molly Ryan and were asking their street girls if they had been approached by any weirdo's or anyone that seemed to put them on edge, but they knew that at least one minder was always in the background so none of them could help out that way.

" Look girls," said Ron, "you are all well protected by our boys that you all know well, and if any punter seemed iffy, just give the nod and he will be taken care of by one or two of the boys and won't bother you again, that's for sure.

The Hooper's had a biddie topped shortly after Molly was killed in just the same way as well, so if anything should happen again, not necessarily on our manor, I'll meet with Bert, he is the brainy one of the two, and between us we will find him and sort out our own Justice, so carry on as normal girls and don't be frightened."

Lucrecia spoke up and said, "Any little squeak or whisper you girls might hear, tell me, Ron or a minder and we will take care of it, your safe girls, that's all for now, go about your business."

In the police canteen Roger asked Jack what he knew of the Ravenhill's and the Hooper's.

He had heard they were hardened villains but wondered about their backgrounds.

"O.k. here is what I know for sure," said Jack, "They were both in the Essex regiment as national service many years ago, and during that time they became great mates while they were in the army, both in Hong Kong and Korea, but even there they ruled the roost, they always picked on some poor sod that was doing his best to keep out of trouble, even the officers kept their distance.

But there was one soldier in particular they singled out, I believe his name was Somerville, a very quiet lad that wouldn't say boo to a goose, and who could have been taken for a choir boy, they often had him in tears and not only forced him to give them his small wages or take a beating, they got him on almost permanent Jankers, it was them that first called him 'jankers Joe.' I believe the poor sod finished up in a psychiatric ward.

Then Ron Ravenhill threatened to throw one officer over the side of the mountain and had to be held back, then he broke his colonel's jaw and got thrown out of the army with a dishonourable discharge, while Hooper used his loaf, done his two years in the army, then with his brother Bill, who somehow dodged his call up started their big life of crime, both are well known to everyone in the Met.

Bill has been in the slammer a few times as he has a short and vicious temper, especially when he has had a few whiskeys, Bert was a former champion cage fighter who somehow had his foot broken, and now has his finger in many pies, as well as promoting his own shows, they worked their way up and much this side of the Thames and some of the other is "their territory," as they call it."

Jack stopped for a cigarette before continuing, The "Ravenhill brigade," as they are known, rule the east side of the river with a rod of iron, his sister fights better than a lot of men, so if you have problems with her at any time, make sure she is handcuffed first, and I do mean that mate."

Roger Osborn smiled saying, "Yes guv. It's a bit different to Berkhamsted, or Berko. as it is known, but this is what I want to do and hopefully I won't make mistakes along the way, although I am sure you will keep an eye on me in that score."

Looking across the canteen, one of Jack's old mates called out to him, waving back he said to Roger, "That's an old mate who took me on when I was just a rookie cop, his name is Alex Ford and he taught me many of the tricks and wrinkles I'm going to teach you, he works in the stores now as he is officially past it, but has always been such an asset the top brass keep him on, he is always cheerful and if you need anything or lose anything, Alex is the man to see.

He is a big softy at heart, and for all his size he is just like a big teddy bear, he was once a children's entertainer and they all loved him.

He was once chosen to run for the Great Britain sprint team, but before he could do that he was caught up in a bank raid and got shot in the hip, then his wife walked out on him saying he put his job before her and that hit him pretty hard, although she may well have been right in that respect, as the job has always been his life, but they remained friends and if she needed help he is always there for her, I guess that's what love does to some people, but the job always was his world and still is, when he has to really retire I don't know what he will do, If he had his way he would stay in the force till he died, even now he has to wear tinted glasses as bright lights cause him to have painful migraines."

Later in the day, after an exhaustive but fruitless time spent visiting clubs and bars for any type of lead they decided it was time to go home.

Jack was beginning to warm to his new partner and was pleased to be invited to dinner on the following Sunday to meet his family.

Jack had settled down to watch a late night movie when his phone rang. Picking it up, he listened and became alert straight away. "Are you sure about that?" he said, "I know, it's low key at first, but when the media finds out his name they will have a ball, call Sergeant Osborn and tell him I will meet him at the yard in 25 minutes, thank you."

Checking his watch he saw the time was just after 2.a.m. "This has got to be too much of a coincidence," he thought, "It's beginning to look like a serial killer is on the loose."

In the briefing room at Scotland Yard they were told the murdered man was a well-known politician.

Sir Rupert Smyth-Saxon, who was on various committees for gay rights marches, same sex marriages, legalised brothels etc. and was outspoken in what he believed to be the rights of the people that had elected him, he was often seen on television and in the news and always spoke up in parliament.

And now he had been murdered in his own flat dressed in woman's clothing and wearing full make up and a wig.

The police operator that took the recorded call played it back to the officers in the room. It came through in a disguised muffled voice saying. "This is not a hoax, I have just strangled a member of parliament, I am phoning from his flat, and by the time you can find this address, I shall be long gone, keep searching."

The officer in charge told those present they had located the address within five minutes, but by the time the response car had arrived there was no one in the vicinity, and it was now put in the hands of the two detectives.

Leaving two uniformed officers at the flat entrance, Jack and Roger entered the spacious room with the on duty doctor, who examined the body saying. "I would say he was strangled from behind, but as there is no sign of forced entry to this flat or broken door lock, it is fairly safe to assume that he knew his attacker and was probably expecting him, but that is your department my friends, I will arrange for the body to be moved within the next twenty minutes or so."

Then with a cheery wave to the two men, he left the room.

"We start with normal procedure," stated Jack. "Check his diary for anything to show any visitors today, last week or any that is due within the next few days, I'll check out his computer, very often something shows up on it, and in the morning the lab. boys will have it in pieces to see if anything is of use to us."

"Well guv." Said Roger, "His diary was full of appointments for all of last week at his surgery, many are complaints against the council, marked in red, with names and addresses, mostly about not enough Parking spaces, some in green that he can give answers to about bus services etc. and general moans in blue, saying he is no help at all, and there is one for tonight in pink, but no time or name, just a big question mark! that could be interesting, have you had any luck with his computer?"

Jack nodded saying, "A little so far mate, but mainly photos of his holidays that we must check out, some with discretion that must be given the all clear by our boss, as a few married M.P.'s pop up that could cause a stir the house of commons, I am sure there will be more than one or two of them worrying and wondering what will come to light once it makes national news, also many of himself in his cross-dress poses, but those won't interest us, its names and faces we want mate!"

Roger added,"It's getting serious now sir, I mean guv. another 2.a.m. murder, the papers will say he's laughing at us, and we can't do a thing as we've very little to go on so far, and they are right."

Jack shook his head saying, "We have started Roger mate, we know he is a big man, a six footer at least, as poor old Rupert had a large neck and was about fifteen stone, so no light weight could have strangled him with their bare hands, and one thing more the doctor has told me is that our killer is probably left handed, just possibly ambidextrous as the poor girls' had their throats cut from right to left, meaning the left hand started the cut from the opposite side, gruesome I know mate, but things like that you pick up as you go along."

The following morning their boss had them in his office again to find out just how it happened and to check their reports.

He told them he had the lab boys working on the computer hard drive, and they had discovered that the Hooper twins had offered him their full time protection some three months earlier if he felt he needed it, as a whisper was going round he might just have a 'nasty accident' at any time.

He laughed at them, telling them he had police protection if and when needed. They got back to him and said the offer still stands, as some of his long term parliamentary colleagues were on their books, and they were still willing to negotiate terms with him.

It appeared he dismissed it and sent no reply back, so make them your first call, it's getting out of hand Jack, I'll leave it to you both do and say what needs to be done, just don't tell me till it's done."

Jack smiled at Roger saying, "This will be an experience for you mate, Bert will listen, take in and remember, but Bill can be fine one minute and threatening the next, I have crossed paths and swords with them both over the years, and for villains they keep their manor under control.

They are known as 'The Enforcers,' many celebs. like to be seen in their company, something like the Kray twins were, only now more up market, so we go to see them now and see what they can tell us, if it suits them.!"

At the main gates the controller knew they were coming and were given permission to go through to the main doors, even there, one of their team checked their car over thoroughly before they got out.

The gangster nodded and pointed to the front double doors and walked in close behind them. Bert greeted them like long lost friends, giving them a beaming smile and ushered them into well laid out room, complete with all mod cons and a large well stocked bar.

"I trust this is a social call Jack? I hope you don't mind me calling you that, as we have known each other a long time, it's a shame Bill's not here, but he's out on a bit of business, if you know what I mean? and if I am not mistaken, your sergeant's name is Roger Osborn, married with two children and recently moved to London from a small town in Hertfordshire!"

Roger stepped forward, but before he could say anything Jack put his hand up and stopped him.

"Partly social and partly business," said Jack, "You know it's off the record anything you tell me Bert, but don't give me any old bullshit, you are usually the first to get any whisper of what goes on in your line of business, especially on your ground, so what gives with the girls' murdered on your manor? And the right honourable sir Rupert, the Member of Parliament got his last night as you must have heard, or did you already know?" Bert lit his favourite Havana cigar before answering saying, "Sure we heard the old fool got the chop last night, it serves him right, as if he had been under our wing, he would be alive today, you know our methods Jack, he wasn't a 'ginger beer' mate, he just liked dressin' up in tarts clothes like some do, we only go for geezers that have got the wonga, we don't turn over banks or security vans anymore and never put pressure on those that can't afford it, 'cos we were like that as kids ourselves once, we know, and you know we aint do gooders, and never will be, but don't think about trying to pin anything on us 'cos Billy boy will come down on you and your mate like a ton of bricks, and I wouldn't try to stop him! apart from that, we know nothing, we settle our own scores, now get the hell outta here before I lose my temper."

Jack looked him straight in the eye as he replied with no show of fear.

"Don't you try to scare us off Bert, you know that won't work, we are looking for answers not fall guys or scapegoats, and if Billy boy tried that I would kick him so hard in the crutch he will have to change his name to Belinda, you may well be holding out on us, if you are, I will find out and we will be back officially and nick you for withholding vital information, we are calling on the Ravenhill's now, maybe they will be more open than you are."

As they left, Bert called out, "Piss of, and don't come back unless you've got a search warrant!"

"You done the right thing by keeping quiet Roger," said Jack, "I know how to handle his type, It's mostly hot air unless he means it, then he is one rough handful, I've seen him perform in cage fights and he was, and still is an animal when he to needs to be, I know the Ravenhill's as much as the Hooper's mate, hard as nails to anyone who gets on the wrong side of them, so even trying to get just one person to testify against them rarely happens, those that are still alive and have done so, still live in fear and have changed their minds before going to court, but they are soft hearted where charities are concerned and both give generously to them, so they are generally always one or two steps ahead of the law, they always look after their own and both knew blind Ted, so unless we get the shitehawk that killed poor old Ted before they do, he will wish we had got him first mate."

Twenty minutes later they arrived at the Ravenhill's main gambling and strip club. Jack said, "It's called 'Rick's Place,' as he liked the film "Casablanca,"starring Humphrey Bogart, So that's how it got its name, Just useless information really, but you might have wondered why, and knowing him pal, he will be expecting us! You can't mistake him, he's got eyes like a shithouse rat and he doesn't miss a trick."

Chapter 3

One of the heavies on the door took the two policemen through to Ron Ravenhill's office and they were greeted with a warm handshake and a big smile as he said, "What kept you boys? I half expected you to be here a lot earlier, have you been to seen the Hooper's first? They are the real villains," he said laughing. "Now let's get down to business Jack! Cobblers to the politician that got topped, I couldn't give a monkies if he wore a brimless boy scouts hat and high heeled shoes, any whisper about who killed poor Molly Ryan? you know in a way she was special to me, more than just a hooker as she was a nice kid, but with me business is business as you know, and she served her purpose but I want a name mate,! if we had not let her go freelance she would still have had our protection and would be alive today, if you know who it might be tell me now and the bastard is mine, then you can have what's left of him, that won't be much, but I promise you he will suffer first."

Jack listened to what Ron said before answering him saying, "This is official Ron, this is my sergeant Roger Osborn, who takes notes of anything you might know yourself that will help us find the killer, but give you a name! well you know I couldn't do that even if I had one, Bert Hooper said much the same thing to us, although so far we don't have a lot to go on but it's early days yet, and it's high profile now that M.P.s got the chop, you know I won't leave no stone unturned on this one, and who ever I upset won't bother me in the slightest, Lucrecia and your boys may see more of us than usual, just don't try to do our job for us Ron, we will even the score for Molly I surely promise you that, and your name was never in the frame for this one."

Ron gave a half smile saying, "We are law abiding citizens, perish the thought that we would even dream of being less than that!"

On their way back to blind Ted's tower

block Roger asked, "You're in with the top villain's guv' how come you get along with them so well? do you really trust them to be truthful."

"Well mate," he replied. "My dear old dad was a copper and I idolised him, even though I was brought up in a not so posh area, dad taught us kids right from wrong, he never hit us, or anything like that, he didn't need to as mum and dad had our greatest respect, we had really loving parents, I saw other kids try drugs and shoplifting, joining street gangs with guns and knives and many went to borstal or prison, some died young, but we were very lucky family wise, and I followed dad's advice and joined the 'Bill' to hopefully be as good as he was, so I grew up with all types and in this line of work, I see some of them now and again," then with a grin said, "And again and again."

After knocking on a few doors, mostly without reply, they called on Ted's old mate Sid who had seen him just before he died, who told them although he did not see anyone, he heard a loud knocking on a door as he went down the stairway but did not look back, and it may have been someone at Ted's front door, but that was all he knew.

Roger said, "Somebody must have seen something or someone surely guv? it was the middle of the day, are people really that frightened to come forward and speak up?"

"You're learning fast Roger mate," said Jack, "On these kinds of estates you will find that people see nothing and hear nothing, Sometimes someone will come forward after a month or so, but we want answers now mate!"

The following morning's newspapers again headlined the murdered politician's cross-dressing life style.

One newspaper that always hit the headlines with the latest scandals hinted there were others in parliament just the same with much to hide, and had received tapes and photographs showing just who some of them were.

They said they had been sent to them

anonymously, but had been given a high court order not to print pictures or names. The paper concerned is appealing against the gagging order, and in large bold letters have a heading, "WATCH THIS SPACE."

Back at Scotland Yard, Roger Osborn was called to the commissioner's office and was told that good reports had come through on how he was a recognised marksman with a shotgun, and was asked if he would like to go on an advanced armed response course that was for seven days with different types of guns, to which he jumped at the chance and was told he would start the following morning.

Also Jack Farley was a member of that elite squad and had recommended him, as he was composed under pressure. Jack just smiled when Roger told him about it and just said, "If I didn't think you were up to it I would not have recommended you for it, and you would not be my sergeant, as I need someone that I can rely on under pressure, and I think you are that man mate! and for the next seven days I shall have the odd constable now and then for back up till you return if needed, so go for it pal, and I will see you in a weeks' time!"

Lucy Rainbow looked at her watch and saw it was five minutes to two a.m. on a dull overcast morning, she was pleased with herself knowing that she had earned £250 for a busy evenings work, even Lucrecia Ravenhill will be happy with that she thought, "And it's £50 for myself, not bad at all, the room he rented was grotty, but it was obvious he was married and wanted a bit of rumpo on the side, maybe he wasn't getting any at home."

She smiled to herself as she turned to wave at her minder before putting the key in the lock to her flat, but he was nowhere in sight!

She felt a moment of panic as she hastily tried to get the key in the lock but dropped it in fright.

As she bent down to pick it up a voice from behind her spoke quietly saying,

"Lost your key Lucy darling? I'll find it for you!"

Looking up startled, she saw a familiar face and breathed a sigh of relief saying, "You had me worried for a moment, you was here only this afternoon darling, do you want more? come back tomorrow lover boy, I am too tired for naughties right now."

The man's voice grew stronger as he said, "You call every one of your clients darling, but you don't mean it! That's what you called me this afternoon, and it didn't mean a thing to you, if it had been for real, I wouldn't have needed to kill you now."

He pulled her roughly to him, putting a gloved hand over her mouth to prevent her from screaming and whispered to her, "I am the 2 a.m. killer, I followed you and your minder after I left you this afternoon, he was useless and did not know I followed his every move until a few minutes ago, then I slit his throat, the same as I will do to you."

He gave a harsh laugh as he said,

"My, my, it's 2.a.m. time to join your minder now!"

Lucy tried to break free, but stood no chance as the knife sliced into her neck killing her instantly.

And as silently as he came her killer disappeared into the night. But not before he purposely dropped a polka dot scarf some 20 yards away.

The scarf belonged to one of a gang of illegal immigrants who thought they were beyond the law, and being deported to where they came from was a joke to them, as inside a week they would be back in this country.

An early morning milkman made the two gruesome discoveries of the bodies on his rounds and in no time the area had been taped off awaiting the arrival of D.C.I. Jack Farley and his latest temporary assistant.

A number of police officers were on hand, and the scarf had been found and taken away for forensic evidence, also a small tent erected for the doctor to do a preliminary examination.

Jack knew that the public would be very nervous once this murder became known and he knew they had every right to be, also questions would be asked in both houses of parliament, mainly by those members with something to hide, Jack mused.

He also knew the Ravenhill Brigade as they were known by, would be up in arms losing Lucy Rainbow and her minder, and would be thirsting for blood and revenge, for that to happen means losing face and showing weakness unless immediate retaliation happens, and unless he could do anything to stop it, it could mean gang warfare on the streets of London.

Lucrecia had heard the commotion and quickly came on the scene.

"Well Chief Inspector Farley, how nice to see you back here again so soon, is it crumpet or gambling you're after? we have everything you need!"

"Don't be sarkie with me Lucrecia, "snapped Jack, "Where is Ron right now, and don't give me any old crap! If he's not here he'll be in big trouble, so where is he?"

" He's gone to do the job you should be doing right now mister policeman, you just ride around scratching you arse and doing sod all, well we aren't the type of people to sit around and watch our own get killed by some nutter your lot can't find, we fight fire with fire, so piss off and get stuffed."

"You stupid great cow," Jack exploded, "If he's gone to turn over the asylum seekers I'm bloody sure he's got the wrong end of the stick, that scarf was a plant and whoever did it has his head screwed on and knows just what to do, he's a real pro. but we'll get him Lucrecia, what we don't need is gang warfare on the streets, how many innocent people will get killed needlessly? you get him on the phone and tell him to hold fire till I get there, if it is them I will nick the bastards myself, listen, we went to school together as kids, and although Ron was the hard nut, he was never a bully, he got in with the local villains and proved his worth to them by taking them on at their own game, and after his national service, he soon became the top banana and you joined him, you are what I call, for want of a better description, 'good villains' but if you cross that line, I won't give a monkies who you are, and you'll both go down for a long stretch, that I promise you, so get him on your mobile now!"

Lucrecia looked at Jack and said, "O.k. Jack, but if you're wrong, remember we play just as rough, and we've got no rule book to follow!"

Less than a minute later she had her brother on the phone telling him Jack Farley needed to talk to him.

Handing him the phone she said, "Say it quick Jack, 'cos he's in no mood for fancy talk, and when he's like that hell an' high water won't stop him!"

"Listen to me Ron," Jack said, "Don't go in mob handed yet, give me your exact location and I'll be there A.S.A.P. if I'm wrong then do what you have to, but hear me out first, o.k.?"

After 30 seconds Ron Ravenhill replied,

"O.K. jack, but this is a one off, don't ever expect me to do this again!"

He gave his location and 15 minutes later he was standing by the Docklands light railway in the East End of London trying to explain to Ron his reasons for a set up.

"Listen mate," he said. "That lot would not go about it that way, for a start it would have been a knife in the back or in the heart, that's mainly their way of killing, and your boy would have sussed him or them out very quickly before it all happened and would have got help from your team straight away, I am sure it is the work of one nutter, for whatever reason he has against street girls I don't yet know, that scarf was a plant for you to fall for, and you have mate, if you start a gang war now he will become a really dangerous serial killer, and as well as catching him I will be after you and anyone else involved if I had too, I wouldn't want to, but by hell I will!"

"You may be right Jack," said Ron, "I thought the same thing about the scarf, but even getting rid of some of this scum

47

that get away with their 'No-speaka-da-english' cobblers can't be a bad thing, you know more about this case and what's happening than I do, but I'll give you one week to sort it out then you come looking for me, 'cos we aint holding back, and we'll follow our own set of rules."

"That's not long enough Ron, make it a month" replied Jack.

"No way mate, two weeks at most," replied Ron, "Then the chips are down and you can tell that to your boss at Scotland Yard!"

Jack knew where the asylum seekers hung out, they called themselves 'The Euros' and they were not afraid of the law.

They knew that they could get away more easily with their criminal activities in the U.K. than in their own country where they would more than likely be shot.

He also knew their top man was originally from Kosovo, and in his own country was a wanted killer whose name was Marco Perez, or was at the moment, as he had used so many aliases' no was sure of his real name.

Jack had parked his police car at the nearest police station and walked the grimy back streets to their last known headquarters, telling the officer in charge at the police station that under no circumstances to send back up.

As jack reached the address he was looking for the door opened before he could knock, and a pock marked man with a long scar on his face spoke in broken English, "Maya be the bossa man no wont to seea you mister policeman, 'cosa we knowa who you are!"

Jack purposely looked at him scornfully and said, "Take me to him now sunbeam, and don't give me any lip or I'll bust you in half, you're an underling, I don't deal with the likes of you, so get with it!"

The pock marked man said, "Followa me, I notta forgeta youa, in my country I woulda killa youa and thinka nothing of ita."

"In your dreams." said Jack as they went into a semi dark room.

Marco Perez spoke first saying, "You must excuse the lighting chief inspector Jack Farley, you see I know who you are and why you are here, you are correct in thinking the two killings you are investigating have nothing to do with us, and you have avoided unnecessary bloodshed with the Ravenhill mob, you see inspector I have spies everywhere!" "If you're that clever Marco," said Jack, "Perhaps you can tell me who the killer is, but you're not that clever! I know you have a team of pickpockets ranging from small kids to women with pushchairs who prey on the elderly and unsuspecting, and it means nothing to you if you stole a blind persons last penny, as you say, you have spies everywhere, also I know one of your gang has been following me since I left the Ravenhill mob, he was very amateurish and so obvious, and if that punk on your door fancies his chances I will accommodate him any time. I am here to warn you to not get involved in any way with our investigations, because if you do, I will come down on you and your gang like a ton of bricks, I don't like you or your kind Perez, and the sooner you are put away the better, I'll find my own way out." Jack said and turned and left the room.

Knowing the killer was always one step ahead of them, Jack had to accept he was unable to take time off, even though he had made arrangements and had planned the outing with Sylvia and Emma.

That evening he phoned Sylvia Star to explain why he had to cancel the following day due to the pressures of his work, and asked her to tell Emma he would make it up to her the next time they meet up.

"I understand Jack," she replied, although he could tell she was disappointed, your job must come first, it always has!"

Jack put the phone down, lit a cigarette and thought to himself, "Sometimes I think I have missed out somewhere along the line."

But knew in his heart he was not a pipe and slipper man and went over his notes again.

Chapter 4

It was a well-known fact that Sir Hugo Bland was 'gay,' and that although a member of the House of Lords he liked to be seen in the company of younger men, he chuckled as he used to say. "Dear boy, they make me feel young again myself."
It was way past midnight when he took a cab home from the "Hello Sailor" gay bar, having given his latest 'boyfriend' the key to his apartment and told him he would be along in about an hour, just be ready for when he returns.
He paid off the taxi outside his mews apartment and thought how lucky he was to live in the heart of the west end and be so close to all the amenities he had been used to all his life, his schooling had been at a top university and it was there that he realised other boys interested him more than any of the girls, and soon realised he was not alone in that way of thinking.
He hummed a tune as he opened the apartment door and was surprised to see a

vaguely familiar face smiling at him.
How did you get in here?" he asked,
"And where is my friend Tarquin? get out
now before I call the police!"
The cruel look in the other person's eye
made Hugo shudder with fear as he said,
"If it's money you want, there's a £1,000
in the wall safe, take it all and I won't
mention to anyone you have been here.
The other man stood up and said. "Don't
you want to see your friend Tarquin,
Hugo? he's in the bedroom, come with
me."
Grabbing Hugo by the shoulder he pulled
him into the bedroom, and Hugo gave a
scream as he saw Tarquin's body
sprawled out on the bed covered in blood
with his throat cut from ear to ear.
"Why does that? "Blubbered Hugo,
"He never did you any harm."
"Your kind are vermin"! Snarled his
attacker, "You've probably guessed I am
the 2 a.m. killer, and your next!"
"No, please don't kill me, I promise not
to say anything to anyone, don't kill me
please, I beg you."

Slapping him hard across his face, the killer said, "My, my, it's five minutes past two, I am late this morning and with one clean sweep Hugo's neck was sliced open.

Checking no one was around, the man with the slight limp made his way to his car whistling as he went.

The following morning the national papers headlines were, "The 2.a.m. killer strikes again." "Is no one safe from the new "Jack the ripper"? Politicians or prostitutes, he cares not for whatever status, he must be caught, and the police seem powerless to do anything about it. The met. is the largest force in the country and they have come up with nothing so far."

Early that morning Jack was called into his chief's office and was told to waste no time and pull out all the stops. The top brass would look the other way as to his methods, but he must get results, either through his underworld associates, narks or shake downs if necessary. Strong questions were being asked in parliament that needed answering, and he had to come up with something.

"Look Jack," his chief said, "This killer is taunting us, he is either very clever or doesn't give a damn if he is caught, but the public are up in arms, we are getting nutters phoning in saying they are the man we are looking for, and we have to check each one out, some walk in to reception saying, It's me, I confess. It's a waste of man power Jack, if anyone can crack this one, you can, but we need results fast!"

"I'll do my best sir," replied Jack, "It will get my best shot."

Back in his office Jack had three messages on his answer phone, the first he discarded immediately from a crank caller claiming to be the killer, but the second and third held his attention.

He listened intently as a woman's voice clearly said. "My name is Carol Mortensen and I am a professional psychic, I read tarot cards, etc, before you decide to cut me off listen to what I have to say, my professional name is "Opal

Lady," and I am a physic and medium,
I am Danish by birth and have helped the
Danish police on a number of their cases,
of which I am sure they will confirm if
you contact them, I am not out to make
money, as in this case I would not ask for
any fee, I want to see this killer brought
to justice.
I will leave my mobile phone number
with you should you wish to reply to this
message."
The next message said. "Your reception
officer informs me you are out of your
office, but one thing I will say that is not
mentioned on the news or in the papers is
that for some reason; the killer sometimes
wears a uniform of some description!
I travel to various countries a great deal,
so contact me before the week end as I
will be leaving for a month in Australia,
if you think I can be of assistance to you,
regards Opal Lady."
"The woman is good," thought Jack,
"There is no way she could have known
that by guess work, but I don't want it
made known to the public yet, I'll call

her now and arrange a meeting."

Opal Lady had an office in a discrete mews just off Oxford Street and hardly known to the general public, and as Jack paid off his taxi fare he had a premonition that he was being followed, and as a rule his sixth sense was usually right.

Looking round he could see no suspicious characters near the mews and made his was Opal Lady's office, showing his police badge on the entrance video,

he again looked all round as the hairs on the back of his neck tingled.

Seeing no one in sight he made his way to Opal Lady's office.

She was a slightly built lady with a charming smile and greyish eyes that seemed to be able to tell what you were thinking.

"Sit down chief inspector and I will tell you what the tarot and cartomancy cards have to say, firstly the man you are looking for is sixtyish.

The first card I drew was the king of cups reversed, showing him to have been in authority at one time but not so much now, he is able hide his emotions by putting on a cheerful face but only for so long, the next card was the five of wands reversed, showing a uniform of some kind, but I cannot say what type, although it is a demotion of some kind, perhaps in the territorial army or cadets of some kind, maybe even boy scouts, there are so many possibilities for that, I could not be positive, and would not hazard a guess, but I get a strong feeling that this man may well have a habit of cracking his knuckles when trying to control his temper.

That card was 'The Fool, reversed, and my advice to you is to be very careful, this man is extremely dangerous.

Now I will turn a couple of cards for you Chief Inspector.

once, ordinary playing cards I use for cartomancy and one deck for tarot, your first card turned Although I often use two decks of cards at over is the Joker upright, it shows you to have a sense of humour, although at times you are unconventional and prefer to do your own thing, the next card for you was 'The Hierophant,' and that shows you recognise right from wrong and will not be swayed by what other people say of think, but you will speak your mind and not always say what is expected of you. For yourself, you have strong, sensitive hands with good intuition, but your vibes tell me something else is bothering you at this moment in time, would you care to say what it is?"

Jack replied, "Yes Opal Lady, I had the feeling that I was being followed but saw no one, so I will phone now and make sure two plain clothed officers are close by until you leave for Austrailia, I will o.k. them when they arrive one at a time as if they were clients and leave you then, you will be safe."

Within an hour the two officers arrived 15 minutes apart as prospective clients, and Jack went back to his office after telling Opal Lady to make no house calls if asked to by phone and to call him if she should get any.

An hour later she called Jack to say she had a call asking her to visit as the caller said he was a housebound invalid and could not travel, she told him she could give him a reading over the phone but he wanted her to call, on asking his address he put the phone down.

Jack thanked her, and immediately got on to the telephone company who traced the call and informed him that the call was from Picadilly underground tube station, not a private address, Jack knew it was useless sending anyone there as he would be long gone.

Back in the canteen sipping a cup of tea his old friend Alex Ford joined him and said, "Well Jack mate I hear you have a lady friend you are sweet on and that she has a little girl called Emma who….."

"Who told you that?" Jack said sharply, "My personal life is nothing to do with my job!"

"Simmer down Jack mate," Alex said with concern, "You know that Scotland Yard is no different than any other nick, everyone knows who's got a bit on the side and who's humping who, and who the gays are, there are a few ginger beers here who must be wondering who's next on the list and keeping their doors locked and bolted at night!"

He gave a chuckle at that and said, "No one told me Jack, it was said by a couple of W.P.C.'s walking past the stores the other day, but if you have, then I wish you every happiness for the future."

"Sorry about that mate," answered Jack, "But Sylvia and myself are just good friends, and Emma is a lovely little girl who calls me Uncle Jack."

Standing up he said, "Things to be done Alex, I must go now, let me know if you hear a whisper, see you later pal."

Later that evening Jack had a phone call from his former sergeant, Nick Stone who was on a special course in America visiting the down sides and dregs of New York, Chicago, Detroit and Harlem. Now that he was a Metropolitan Police Superintendent, having passed his examination with flying colours he was given the chance to see first-hand the low life of the big cities and how the New York and American police handle the many situations they meet every day, and possibly integrate some of their ideas into U.K. Policing.

"You've got your work cut out there guv. there I go again," said Nick, "You will always be guv. to me, it's a force of habit Jack mate, you were my boss for so long I won't change now, but from what I've seen on T.V. and read in the papers the killer is a real pro. but my feeling is he is not a professional hit man, it's someone with a personal grudge against hookers and homosexuals and a person that knows London well, I would say we are looking for someone with inside knowledge that others can't get at and that narrows the field down a bit, but that is just my opinion mate! It could be someone in the force, or has been at one time, or a civil servant that can see classified information and unfortunately some private security companies are given the info. first."

"Jack grinned as he said, "You must have

read my thoughts Nick, I am working on those lines myself, just two more days and you will be back in England again and you have been given a cushy number, stationed at Richmond-on-Thames police station, then the following month you get married to the lovely Candy, I am really pleased for you both Nick, it turned out well in the end, will speak to you again soon Nick, 'bye for now."

The following morning Jack was out early in the morning to find a few of his 'narks' that might have heard anything of importance, he preferred an unmarked car and liked to keep a low profile when he made those visits.

Firstly waterloo station, but nothing, then Euston station, still no joy and then the other main line station at St. Pancras and still no luck.

Then finally going to kings Cross station where he met one of the not so reliable squeaks known as 'Nicky The Nark' who sometimes told him things that he never would have found out without a grass, and at other times rubbish he had made up himself.

"I fink I can 'elp yer out a bit on this one guv'nor," he said, "But I aint got the price of a cuppa, let alone a sandwich, 'an I know you've always been good to me, so if I shows yer what I found will yer give me a fiver.?

"Where, and what did you find Nicky?" said Jack, "I haven't got time to play any games, so don't give me any old crap or I will sort you out myself then pass you on to the transport police, and you know they have their own methods of dealing with you lot, and I won't help you if you try to con me, so put up or shut up right now"!

Nicky looked all round as far as he could see and said, "All right guv. keep yer bleedin'shirt on, it's fer real I tell yer, yer know that biddie that got topped in Trafalgar square the other night,? well I just 'appened to be there havin' a 'Jimmy Riddle' behind one of them lions statues when I heard a scream, and a man's laugh as he said, "Serves yer right you cow, your just like the rest of 'em, then he moves away sharpish an' it looked like he had a bit of a limp the way he moved, does that 'elp yer guv.?"

"It might," replied Jack, "But what did you find? and don't give me any of your bullshit, just show me what you found now, and it had better be good.!"

Nicky looked round the station again nervously as he pulled a dirty handkerchief out of his pocket and said, "Here it is guv."

And opening his handkerchief showed half a blade of a cutthroat razor.

Jack looked at him as he put on a pair of rubber gloves and taking the half blade from him and said, "You stupid fool, rather than give you a fiver, I should run you in for withholding vital police evidence, and what D.N.A. there might have been you've destroyed, you bloody pillock! You must have stood right by the girl when you picked it up, why didn't you check her out or call the police or at least tell someone there had been a murder! I'm taking you to the nick right now and you can make an official statement there and you'll be lucky if you don't get a long spell in the slammer because of this!"

"Sorry guv'nor," Nicky said, "I didn't fink about that, as I always pick up odds and ends, like any coins I see, or train tickets that come in useful, an' I could tell the biddie was dead straight away, so I scarpered there an' then."

Jack wanted to punch him, but firstly said, "She was no biddie Nicky, just a poor woman that never had the breaks that others get, so never call her that again!"

Back at Bow police station where Jack had taken him, he made him go over all he had said earlier and anything else he could remember.

But Jack had the feeling that Nicky was holding something back, either he had seen the killer and was scared, or thought he might a few pounds if he waited till the next day and had a night in the cells that were more comfortable than a station bench that usually meant getting moved on anyway, even after one and a half hours he stuck to the same story.

Jack let him spend the night in the cells as he wanted, but warned him not to think he could con his way along,, or he would turn him over to the railway police, and no way had Nicky wanted that, and that Jack would see him again later the next day.

Shortly after twelve midday, Roger Osborn reported that he was back from his firearms course and ready to resume his normal duties.

Jack smiled as he said, "Let's have a cup of tea first Roger,"

And making their way to the canteen Jack said, "I've had good reports on your shooting prowess and that you scored very high marks on all the weapons you used, probably due to living in the countryside, but one thing I need to know, and think about it before you answer as someone's life could depend on it, would you be able to shoot to kill a person if you had no other choice? I'll get the tea and cakes in while you think over the consequences."

Roger was at a loss for words when Jack returned with two teas and a couple of cakes, and sitting down said, "Give me a straight answer mate, any one of us called out could be in the firing line!"

"I hadn't thought of it that way Jack," he replied, "But yes, I would as it would be on my conscience if one of our colleagues was killed because of my wondering should I pull the trigger? If that happened I would blame myself for not doing the job I was trained for."

"Well thought of answer mate, that's what I hoped you would say," Jack said as his old mentor Alex Ford pulled up a chair and sat down.

"Hello Jack my old mate and Roger the newbie," he said, "I hear you are a marksman with guns, not much gets past my cubby hole without me getting to know the score, well done mate, welcome to the club."

Turning to Jack he said, "I hear you've got Nicky the Nark in the slammer at Bow street nick, get back there now and put the screws on him, as he told 'Larry the limp' he saw the killer and was holding out for a big police pay-out and protection, and he would give you a name and all the griff when he gets a fist full of readies off the old Bill, he wouldn't tell the limp who it was, but the limp phoned me just before I came in to see if you were here, so make sure Bow street coppers keep him there!"

"Good grief," said Jack, "I told the desk sergeant to turf him out at 9 o'clock, come on Roger we are off to Kings Cross station to get our man, thanks Alex mate, we're on our way now!"

Alex called out, "Let me know the outcome Jack, I hope it's what you want!"

In a police car with sirens blaring out they raced to Kings Cross station, then ran inside and saw one of the railway police giving directions to a passenger. Jack knew him and said, "Hi Sam, where will I find 'Nicky the Nark'?

The officer looked at him and shook his head. "Haven't you heard Jack? He's dead, the Nark slipped and fell under a tube train about 11o'clock this morning, and he had a half empty bottle of scotch that didn't break! he must have drunk half of it and staggered around, it seems he was three parts pissed and missed his footing, and stood no chance, right under a tube train, their where some witnesses but it's rush hour and they all said much the same, sorry about that mate, but that's how it is."

Jack could have kicked himself for letting him go; his gut feeling was that the nark knew a lot more than he said.

"Where did he get the price of a bottle of whiskey? all he left the nick with was a fiver I gave him, so someone pushed him under that tube train I'd bet my bottom dollar on it, have you got any witnesses addresses Sam?" he asked. "No Jack," he replied, "I wasn't on the underground section today, I am just on the main hall duty, but the boys on duty there tell me no one could help at all really."

"Thanks anyway Sam, but you have been a help, we might see you again soon, 'bye for now."

Chapter 5

On the way back Jack explained to Roger the facts as he saw them, he said, "Firstly he left the nick at 9 a.m. with just a fiver, he got to Kings Cross station about 9.30. still no bottle, saw Lenny the Limp at about 9.45.a.m. chatted till 10 a.m… then who did he meet that gave him a bottle of whisky? I think he was followed from Bow Street to the station by the killer, who waited till he was on his own, then given the bottle that he knew he would start to drink straight away as he knew our man, then taken by some excuse to the underground about 11a.m.where he was pushed onto the line, then the only witness gone, end of story, does that make sense to you Roger?"

"It seems to fall into place guv." said Roger, "but we are no better off unless the close circuit cameras filmed anything, with luck they might have, so we need to see them as soon as possible."

Jack nodded, but said, "I think our man is

too cunning for that to happen mate, he will have made sure he was out of camera range before he made any moves, but we will check it out just in case."

On their return to Scotland Yard they made a point of seeing Alex Ford again to tell him the bad news.

"Check the closed circuit cameras," were his first words, "If he's there, you've got him Jack!"

"They are already being scanned by the S.O.C.O. team Alex, I contacted them straight away, we should hear one way or another soon, right now I want to see your stoolie, Lenny the Limp mate, and he might help a little."

Alex shook his head and said, "He will not tell you anything Jack, he was always my best grass and I was, and still am the only one he would open up to, you would be wasting your time, and all he said to me is what I told you."

"Thanks anyway Alex, but I think I am on to our man's wave length, he is too well informed to be an outsider, maybe he is too cocksure of himself, but I will

nail him before long when he makes more
mistakes, and he will, maybe just small
ones but it will happen, it's the innocent
people he destroys that bug me so much!"
Alex nodded and said," Well make it
soon Jack, the bastard may strike again
soon, and although the guilty ones
deserve all they get, your man is now the
judge, jury and executioner!"
"O.k. Alex, will see you around mate,
we have a lot to do." Jack said.
And with a wave of his arm the two
detectives made their way to the briefing
room to see the commissioner and give
him their report.
After briefly looking at it, their boss said,
"I don't want reports Jack, I want results,
are you getting anywhere? this will do for
the newspapers and T.V. news, but the
P.M. is on my tail each day, if it's not
him, it's one of his cronies, so what is the
score from where you and your sergeant
are now?"
"Slow progress sir, but it's falling into a
pattern that's starting to take shape little
by little, I am trying to put myself in his

shoes as to his next plan of action, and I am sure he has not finished yet, he is definitely a loner and thinks he is untouchable, but we will close in on him as I think he will go way over the top before long, but unfortunately I think he won't be stopped before he kills someone else, that is all I can say so far."

"Alright Jack, I'll leave it with you for the time being, but it's results from now on or someone else takes over the case, that's all for now, keep me informed."

"Not the best of briefings Jack," said Roger, "But I suppose it's more understandable, now that there are some well-known M.P.s that are in the public's eye are getting killed, all parties in parliament will be worried."

"Yes mate, I know, there is something in the back of my mind that I can't put my finger on, I have wracked my brains to pinpoint it but so far no joy, I hope it comes through soon! Anyway Roger, you can go home for a break now, but if you get a phone call I'll be in touch."

At 7 o'clock that evening Jack's phone

rang, Sylvia Starr's voice was frantic with worry, and it was obvious she had been crying.

"Jack, Emma is missing! Someone has taken her, she was in the front garden playing with the little girl next door when I heard a car door slam so I looked out and she had gone, that was five minutes ago, her playmate was crying and said 'a nasty man grabbed Emma and bundled her in a car and said if I said anything he would come back and get me, then drove off,' Help me Jack, please help me I need you here."

"Stay calm Sylvia," said Jack, "I am coming over to you right away, I'll be about twenty minutes if I put my foot down, in the meantime phone your local police station and tell them it's an emergency, and if the little girl she was playing with can describe him it will help a lot, get your neighbour to sit with you till I get there, I am leaving now."

"Please hurry Jack, I don't know what I'd do if he harms her in any way."

Jack could hear her crying as he put the

phone down.

Inside twenty minutes Jack was at Sylvia's cottage and gently coaxed Emma's playmate Donna to try to remember what he looked like and what he said, Jack told her he won't come back, as a policeman will be outside her garden to see he doesn't return.

She told him they were playing a ball game and as the ball bounced over the gate on to the green, Emma went to get it and a nasty big man picked it up and threw it to me, then grabbed Emma and called out if I said anything he would come back and get me!

Jack asked her if she remembered what he was wearing, and was told he had a dark coat on and that his car was a blue one, and that she was scared.

Jack took her in his arms and cuddled her saying, "Don't worry Donna, I promise you he won't come back, your mummy and daddy will see to that."

The local police were making house-to-house calls to see if anyone had seen or heard anything, but no one could help out that way apart from one person who said a blue B.M.W. car drove past his house off the green and onto the road at a fast pace, he knew it was a blue B.M.W. as it was the same as his own car.

Jack immediately put out an all-points bulletin for a blue B.M.W. car in a ten-mile radius.

. He tried to reassure Sylvia that everything that could be done was being done, and that she would be the first to know of any developments, and that he had to return to London due to the case he was on, but that every police force in the country were being notified as of now and he would be on hand whenever possible, although there was no luck with the blue car.

The following morning Jack phoned Sylvia but so far she had heard nothing. But fifteen minutes later Sylvia phoned him back saying, "The 2 a.m. killer has got Emma and sent a letter with a lock of her hair and ribbon in to prove he has her, the letter says, 'Tell Farley to drop this 2.a.m. case or the kid dies, she is not harmed yet, but if I don't see anything in the papers or on T.V. within twenty four hours, my cut throat razor will be busy again! And that is for sure if you want her back again alive, do as I say and I will leave her where you can find her, if not, blame Farley or yourself'."

Jack replied, "Don't handle the envelope any more Sylvia, I am on my way to you now, try not to worry too much my darling, I think I may have the answer to get her back to you, trust me on this one, I am leaving now, see you in about twenty minutes."

A short time later Jack studied the letter that had been typed, also the lock of hair and ribbon that he carefully folded while wearing rubber gloves, and said, "Maybe a small clue on these Sylvia, although I doubt it, but I will give it to the lab. boys to check just in case, and I will tell you what my plan is in case you hear differently, and it does not seem right but this is for you and just a few others who have to be in the know.

It will seem I am suspended forthwith

until further notice for my handling of this case and for insubordination, it will be in the newspapers that another officer will assume my duties, hopefully that will get your darling Emma back and from now on she will be protected."

Sylvia hugged Jack and said, "I don't know what I would do without you Jack, you are my rock."

Jack smiled and said, "Hey now, I'm Uncle Jack, remember?"

Later that afternoon in the commissioner's office Jack outlined his plan to his chief who readily agreed to give it a try saying, "Farley, you are taken off the case as of now, your replacement will take over immediately, it will be chief inspector Desmond Dean and sergeant Osborn will work with him, now take your belongings from that office until an inquiry has been held regarding your conduct, you will now take over traffic control instead until further notice."

Going back to his office Alex Ford stopped him and said, "Bad new travels

fast Jack, the Chief told someone else and one of the lads heard it and told me,
it will soon be all over the Yard, is it pukka the boss man has suspended you from the case? if so that's not fair!
I'll go and see him now and tell him your worth ten of any of the crowd here mate, if anyone can crack this case it's you, that guy Dean only got where he is now because he went to Eton College, the boss can sack me if he wants to, as I have seen so many good ones, and not so good ones come and go, maybe I should cash my chips in now! but he is wrong to give you the elbow."

"No Alex mate, don't do that, he could be right, as a new face and different approach might be needed, anyway, my pal Nick Stone is back from the States in two days' time, and we have a lot to catch up on and he is getting married soon, so maybe a break will be good for me, so leave it!"

Alex sighed, and said, "O.k. Jack, but any inside ifo. I hear I will let you know, and if you need me at all, you know my phone number."

Roger Osborn had not seen Jack and did not know the suspension was all a set up, and was most upset when he heard about it from one of the officers at the reception desk, he well knew of Jack's reputation for doing things his own way, but did not think it would go this far.

He phoned Jack and arranged to meet him at the fish bar they had been in, and when Jack explained it all to him he was very relieved to hear it was a sham, and that Jack was still on the case in his own way. Although Roger was sworn to secrecy, and not even his new acting chief inspector Dean knew of it, all he had to do was to go along with any new ideas and plans of action he was given to undertake.

The following morning the newspaper headlines were in big bold letters stating. "Has the 2.a.m. killer struck again? Another hooker with her throat cut, but this time by the dome." Also "Be in by 1a.m. or you maybe next! East European call girl slain like the others at 2.a.m."

and others read, "Top cop Farley thrown off the case for showing no results!"

And "Panic at Scotland Yard, was D.C.I. Jack Farley suspended, or removed of his post for lack of arrests?"

Chief inspector Desmond Dean was talking to the examining doctor who said, "This may not be the same man my friend, as the poor victim had her throat cut from left to right unlike all the others, so it is possible you may be looking for a copycat killer, still, I wish you luck."

And giving them both a cheery wave walked out to his waiting car.

A small tent had been erected at the crime scene, with police officers coming and going and the B.B.C. and various television news teams were scurrying round to find the best filming positions and hoping to get an eye witness, but knowing people would be too scared to come forward even if they had seen anything.

One reporter cornered D.C.I. Dean and asked him if he could say what the latest developments were? and why was Chief

Inspector Farley taken off of this case and put on traffic duties?

"Who told you that?" he asked, "Your informant has got the facts wrong, D.C.I. Farley's suspension, if you call it that, was an internal matter and had nothing to do with this on-going case."

Having had very little time to read all the reports, he quickly called Roger Osborn over and said, "This is sergeant Osborn who has been on the case since the first murder, I am sure he can tell you and the public at large how things are progressing, take over sergeant!"

Roger quickly explained that the police were doing all they could and did not want the public to be overly alarmed, just make sure that their doors and windows were locked at night, and to carry on as normal during the day, and should any member of the public be suspicious of something they are unsure of, they should inform their local police station straight away or any policeman they see on the street.

He then thanked the T.V. companies and

press for keeping the public informed of the current situation.

Sylvia phoned Jack Farley at midday to tell him that her little Emma is safe and sound and is in Bow Street police station. She told Sylvia the nasty man that took her did not hurt her at all; he got her a take-a-way meal, then just locked her in a room, and hardly spoke at all till he put her in a car the next day, and stopped near a police station, pointed at it and Said. "Go!"

Chapter 6

Jack was waiting for Sylvia at Bow Street Police Station with little Emma who had already been checked over by the police doctor and was fine, except feeling tired, hungry and wanted her mum!
unfortunately she was unable to give a very good description of the man except he was big; and he cracked his fingers a few times and she was very frightened.
"Mummy," she cried out, and ran to her and gave her a big hug.
"Uncle Jack said he will take us both on The London Eye if you will agree, let us go and do it please mum!"
"Of course we can Emma darling;
if Uncle Jack is free we can go now."
she said laughing and holding Emma's hand.
Jack smiled and said. "I've got my car in the police yard so let's go and get it and off we jolly well go Emma."
Next morning Marco Perez phoned to

make an appointment to see the chief superintendent at Bow Street Police Station.

The desk sergeant told him to call back in the afternoon as the Superintendent was attending a meeting at Scotland Yard and would be gone all the morning.

Always being used to getting his own way straight away, he demanded that a senior officer should see him immediately he called in at the police station.

"There will be an officer to listen to what you have to say sir," the desk sergeant said, "If you give me your name I will have someone in the interview room willing to talk to you."

"My name is Marco Perez," he shouted down the 'phone, "A girl I know from my own country has had her throat cut by the person you can't catch! I want answers fast and I want this person caught and killed, if your pol…" "Hold it right there sir,"said the sergeant, "Do not make threats to kill, and should you do so again you may well be arrested!"

Perez said, "In my country we take an eye

for an eye, and use rough justice."

"You are not in your own country now Mister Perez, remember that, and if you care to call in within the next half hour there will be an officer to witness and record your complaints."

Marco Perez slammed the phone down without replying.

Perez took it as an insult that someone thought they could muscle in on his 'so called' territory.

He had heard of the Ravenhill and Hooper outfits as they liked to be called, but was unsure if they would try anything that would cause gang warfare, not that he minded, as illegal immigrants were ten a penny as and when he wanted them, and if they were told to use guns, then they would use them and they would not dare to say that Marco Perez gave the orders.

Although he had not been in England for a great length of time, his ruthless ways had made quite an impact in the area, and his strong arm tactics forced the clubs and pubs to 'pay' for his protection, those that didn't were hit with fire bombs, or the owner's suffered a severe personal 'accident' and decided it was best to pay for his protection.

He sent two of his most hardened villains to see the Hooper brothers' and two more to 'Rick's Place' to find out if either of their 'teams' were involved in any way with his vice girl's killing, as if they were they would have major problems!

The Hoopers' sent their two back with broken ribs and a note saying, 'Don't send boys' to do a man's job, come over yourself next time.'

Ron Ravenhill took a delight in kneecapping the two sent to scare him, and his note said, 'My sister would have done this, but there were only two of them.' Perez could not afford to lose face and vowed he would make them pay for what they had done.

Alex ford phoned Jack Farley and told him he had heard a whisper from his nark that the gang from Kosovo was planning a Capone style hit on Rick's Place in the next day or two, meaning they were using automatic weapons and also hand grenades that would kill any amount of innocent people who were in the area. Perez knew the Hooper brothers' mansion was out of the question to get into, but he planned on parcel and letter bombs to start with then try to eliminate the two of them, either together or one at a time, as he knew he would lose face in the underworld unless he acted quickly.

His plan was to strike at six o'clock the next morning with automatic rifles and a few hand grenades at 'Rick's Place,' using decoys to block the road should police cars be in the area, as the illegal immigrants had to do that, knowing if they didn't, they would disappear and not be seen again.

Jack thanked Alex, and informed his boss at Scotland Yard who made arrangements immediately that a special squad would be dressed as council workers with road works signs up and have a single line traffic barrier outside 'Rick's Place.'

By midnight everything was in place and it seemed to anyone passing that the council were at road works again.

Ron Ravenhill had been informed and was quite pleased, and thought it funny that the police were protecting his club this time and not raiding it.

But knowing him, Jack knew whatever the outcome, Ron would be prepared for whatever Perez tried and he would wish he had left well alone and stayed on his own patch.

The police were well prepared for any eventuality and had 'stingers' ready to throw across the road a hundred yards before reaching 'Rick's place.'

5.45 a.m. and the city was beginning to come to life, early morning buses and traffic was beginning to build up when three high powered mini buses came racing down the road around sixty miles an hour, they took no notice of the emergency traffic lights on red, or the 'council worker' with his hand up who quickly jumped out of the way as the cars sped past.

At the same time a 'stinger'(a long metal chain with large spikes for puncturing tyres) was thrown across the road causing the first mini bus to spin round and crash into a barrier before turning on its side, the second mini bus swerved hard violently, just missing the crashed vehicle and sent a burst of automatic gunfire through the windows and entrance to the club, no one was injured as that part of the club was kept clear.

But the third mini bus followed instructions and swerved sideways, hitting the upturned bus causing it to catch fire, the five occupants scrambled out into the arms of the waiting police, as did the five in the second bus.

The bus that Marco Perez was in was bullet proof with large metal mudguards that smashed into the police cars that were trying to stop them, sending them spinning into other road users and allowing Perez's mini bus to mix with other traffic and make a clean getaway.

Jack Farley's mobile phone rang minutes later and a furious Ron Ravenhill said, "That's it Farley, this means all-out war, no illegal immigrant is gonna get away

with that! Don't try to soft soap me;
my team are after their blood!"

With that he turned his mobile off.

Jack had his sergeant Roger Osborn with him in a marked police car parked in a side road should they be needed.

Then looking at Roger he said, "The shit's hit the fan mate, put your seat belt on, we're going for Perez!"

Jack knew that if he did not get to Perez first there would be open gang warfare with the Ravenhill team, and most probably the Hooper's joining in for support and with so many illegal immigrants in the country, flare ups would start up in many cities and towns, all it needs is an excuse sometimes.

Leaving the scene quickly, Jack knew London well and was able to take short cuts back to the East End.

Although it meant driving the wrong way down one way streets with plenty of near misses traffic wise as they sped down to the docklands area where Perez had one of his many hideouts.

Without warning, a burst of gun fire came

from one of the derelict buildings that shattered the windscreen causing Jack to pull over to one side as more shots were fired blindly in their direction, Jack said, "Come out this side Roger mate, it's getting lighter now and that makes us easier targets," and his sense of humour made him smile as he said, "I bet you will have a good tale to tell when you get back to Berko. for a visit."

Once settled behind the car, Jack phoned though to police H.Q. for armed assistance.

"Does this mean I am o.k. to fire back guv.?" asked Roger. "To bloody true it does mate, "then added, "Knock one off and you win a cocoanut!"

Within minutes a helicopter came into view and they could hear the sound of police sirens getting louder by the minute as help was on its way.

Roger Osborn closed one eye, took careful aim at a man peering through a broken window, and with his police rifle he fired two single shots, and on the second shot they heard the man scream in pain then saw him clutch his right shoulder.

Roger smiled and said to Jack, "An old trick I learned years ago guv, shoot just to one side, he moves to the other side and bingo, he is in your sights, before that he could move either way if you miss him first time."

"Nice one," said Jack, "I'll remember that for sure, now here comes the cavalry to help us, but that bastard Perez must have heard the chopper and sirens and found another hidey hole, so I can see Ravenhill's mob scouring this area starting today aiming to hunt him down, the main problem is it could get nasty for the genuine immigrants and if the Coopers' join in we have a major job on our hands.

I bet the real killer's having a good laugh at this, and my gut feeling is he is close, if only I could say, 'Yes it's come back to me,' it's something I've forgotten I'm sure mate!"

"Don't blame yourself guv. even you can't remember every little thing you done in the past, even a few weeks back takes some remembering, Anyway the boys in blue are here now, and about a dozen have gone in that old closed down factory, and they are armed to the teeth!" The chopper landed on some waste ground about fifty yards away with some sporadic gunfire being heard.

Jack Farley shook his head in disbelief when he saw Don Grant the American F.B.I. agent he last saw in Miami running towards them.

Diving for cover as more bullets bounced off the cars' bonnet he said, "Hiya limey, looks like you gotta bit of trouble over there, well old buddy, Uncle Sam is here to see you and your sidekick come to no harm."

Fifteen minutes later the all clear was given, and the police rounded up twenty five illegal immigrants, four with flesh wounds but no one fatally wounded.

After writing out their reports Jack and Roger listened to what Don Grant had to say.

He told them it was an exchange visit of

ideas and work practice, Nick Stone had gone state side after his promotion, and he being a special agent had been offered the chance to see how the Metropolitan Police in London worked, and as he was coming over as a wedding guest he jumped at the chance.

The Commissioner of police knew he was a high ranking F.B.I. agent in New York, and asked him if he wanted to see first-hand how his force handled any situation; He was only too pleased to say yes when he heard that jack was on the case.

Leaving a small team of elite police officers to deal with any disturbances that may occur, Jack phoned Ron Ravenhill to inform him that the situation had been dealt with, and although Perez had not yet been arrested, armed police were in the area looking for him so he could call his team off as of now.

Ron just said, "We are looking for him as well!" Then switched his mobile off.

"At least you have some guys that don't pussyfoot around," said the American, "And that's what I like, as yours must be one of the world's easiest police forces going from what I see on T.V. and read in the press, if we acted like that in the states, …well old buddy, you know coz you've been there."

Jack gave a half smile and said, "I know Don, I just wonder if we will ever change, but later on today you must come and meet Sylvia again, and of course her little princess Emma who has heard all about you, and seen pictures of you in the American papers her mum sent home to her."

London's West End 1.55 a.m. A fight is starting outside a night club where four drunken youths and their giggling girlfriends are trying to barge past the two bouncers on the door to get in.

But having no luck, they try kicking and punching one of the doormen to get past him, but he grabs the leg of the nearest yob and twists it round causing him to swear and scream with pain, while his girlfriend is pulling at the doorman's hair until the other bouncer chops her on the back of the neck and she slumps forward hitting her head as she falls down just as the police arrive.

They pull one of the yobs away warning him to move on or get arrested and he staggers to an alleyway close by, then followed by his girlfriend who screams in terror as she sees her boyfriend on the ground with blood oozing from his neck and a tall man standing over him.

The man reaches forward to grab her and slashes out with his cut throat razor as she pulls back screaming, her thin top tears away as the blade of the razor misses her neck and cuts deep into the side of her cheek.

Her scream of agony makes her assailant moves swiftly away as a police officer turns and stops her from collapsing, but does not see the tall man sliding out and mixing with the crowd.

Seeing blood pouring from her face he calls for assistance and a paramedic ambulance is on the scene in minutes. Another officer bends down in the dim ally to help her boyfriend up and realises the warm sticky substance he gets on his hands is blood that is still streaming from the youths neck!

Within twenty minutes D.C.I. Dean and Sergeant Roger Osborn were at the scene followed closely by the police doctor had a small tent put over the ally while he examined the youth's body.

Looking at his watch he said to the two detectives, "It looks like your 2.a.m. killer has struck again my friend, but this time he missed out on the girl and that could probably help you a lot if she saw his face, she is in too much of a shock right now and the paramedics have taken her to St Thomas's hospital where she will have a police guard. Well that's all I can do myself tonight, so I will say night, night to you both and see you in the morning."

Giving them a cheery wave he made his way to a police vehicle waiting to take him home.

After questioning the two doormen and a few others who were there, but so drunk they would say anything for a laugh, they gave it up as they knew it was getting nowhere.

They had police cars and constables in pairs scouring the area, and asked the club owner for the security camera film that covered the club entrance and part of the ally as it may well give them the break they hoped for, he readily agreed and the two detectives took it back to Scotland Yard and went straight to the laboratory to check it out.

"What a let-down" said Roger Osborn, "I don't think this tape has been looked at or checked since it was installed, that was half an hour of 'fog,' even the sound was nothing but crackle, and more crackle."

"I know what you mean sergeant," said the D.C.I. "But in the morning we will go to the hospital and get a statement from the girl, it is quite possible that she saw his face, even in the poor light there it is quite likely."

"Let's hope so sir, this killer needs stopping and the sooner the better." said his sergeant.

The following morning the major newspapers were having a field day.

One said. "Is there no stopping this killer?" Another said. "Youth has neck slashed on night out with friends."

Other papers say. "Someone must be shielding this maniacal killer, come forward now!"

New Scotland Yard released a statement to the general public saying. "Go about your business as normal, everything possible is being done to catch the person or persons concerned, each and every new lead is being investigated, and we are confident of an arrest soon, please do not panic."

Desmond Dean and Roger Osborn visited the girl in hospital the following morning, but were disappointed that she could not say what he looked like, except he had a strong smell of cigars.

They asked the girl if she would say she may well recognise him again, but she was so scared she refused point blank to pretend she might recognise him, and asked them to leave her alone.

Don Grant was unable to see Jack Farley a great deal over the next few days, having to be an onlooker in the way the Met police handled their duties.

In some ways he was impressed with their methods, and in others he knew that New York was a whole different ball game, where even juvenile school children had guns and legal gun shops could be found in abundance, as well as the ones that had the goods if the person had the money!

Chapter 7

Meanwhile, many late night clubs had contacted the police asking for uniformed officers to make their presences felt, and in answer, being told in no uncertain terms that the police were on hand mainly for the disturbance the late-night drinkers' cause, and many of them are under age, and they give the police enough problems without having to be on the lookout for any suspicious characters. Alex Ford phoned Jack and informed him his 'nark' had been told on good authority where Marco Perez was holed up.

"That's great news Alex, but I'm off that case, If you tell Desmond Dean where he's at mate, they can nab him before he does any more harm, he has a good man in Roger Osborn and if he takes a few of the 'heavy gang' with him, that could well stop too much gang warfare and they can bring him in with the minimum of trouble."

Twenty minutes later three armed police

vans made their way to the Docklands address they were given.

The exits were covered as the armed police stormed into the converted building ready to take no prisoners but found little resistance, as the Perez gang had thought they were in hiding safely. Macro Perez attempted to escape though a back exit, but found he was looking down the barrel of Roger Osborn's automatic police rifle and immediately surrendered.

In fifteen minutes the building was declared 'clear.' D.C.I. Dean was well pleased with the result, and when the Commander at the yard congratulated him, he did not say the information was passed on to him by their store keeper.

Nick Stone was settling in nicely at Richmond-On-Thames and had a house bought for him as a wedding present on Richmond Green, paid for by his old friend Jack Farley, who said, "It's only money Nick, it's for you, Candy and the family I hope you are going to start!" Nick protested strongly but Jack said,

"I have all I need mate, what good it is just being in the bank? I am glad I could help."

Three nights later a piercing scream was cut short and a loud splash was heard along the Embankment just as two police officers were crossing Lambeth Bridge, one with his police dog, who ran to the steps leading down to the walkway, while the other radioed for more assistance. Slipping the dogs lead the officer said, "Go find him boy!"

The dog bounded off barking fiercely and suddenly yelped as the two policemen managed to catch up with it; it appeared it had been sprayed with a substance.

"That man had no fear of dogs," Said the officer, "Maybe he's a vet. or a dog breeder, my Butch should have pinned him down, but you can bet your life he's thrown the can in the river, but use your torch just in case he dropped it here somewhere."

Within minutes three response cars arrived, one with another dog handler who quickly picked up a scent and went to the water's edge that was high tide. The river police were closing in and had their spotlights on and could see in the murky water a woman's body.

They acted immediately and in no time had the dead woman on board, she still had her shoulder bag over her arm and a woman P.C. opened it to check for identification even though the contents were wet.

The officer was shocked to see that the victim who had her throat slashed open was a northern member of parliament who had probably decided to take a stroll by the river and see the lights of London by night, and had ended up being another victim of the 2a.m. killer.

The spray can was not found by the p.c. as expected, and an examination tent was quickly erected as D.C.I. Dean and Sergeant Osborn arrived on the scene.

"That will cause a stir in parliament sir," said Roger, "it's got to be the same person I think, but if he thought she was on the game he was well mistaken, she was a well-respected member of parliament."

"Very true sergeant; unless we get a breakthrough soon I don't know what will happen, it will most likely come back on us, Jack Farley doesn't know how lucky he is to be off this case."

Roger Osborn just nodded!

Before long the police doctor arrived with little to do, other to confirm the way she was killed, and that in his opinion it was done by the same person they are looking for.

With nothing more to do he smiled saying, "I'll leave you two gentlemen to look for clues."

Giving them both a cheery wave before getting into the waiting police car to be driven home.

D.C.I. Desmond Dean was not a happy man. He said, "Sergeant, I wish the Commander had given this case to someone else, unless it is sorted soon I will have the rest of them laughing at me behind my back, Jack Farley doesn't realise how lucky he is to be on traffic control, I'd swap with him in a flash if

I had the chance."

Roger Osborn just said. "It's not just down to you sir, this is a priority case and it's down to all of us, a lot of other police personnel are involved and we are all trying to bring this man to justice."

"I know," said Dean, but it will be on my record."

Nothing new happened within the next few days and it appeared the police had no new leads to go on.

There had been talk of bringing in police from other parts of the country to assist in the search for the killer, although the Met. Police Commander did not want that to happen as it would mean that the control would be divided among senior officers, some that would see things differently to others and each one would want their ideas put to use straight away.

At 2 a.m. on a wet, drizzly morning very near Westminster Bridge, a woman walking home from her early morning cleaning job heard heavy footsteps behind her, she turned nervously round and saw a heavily built man some twenty yards behind her walking very fast.

She quickened her pace and turned round again to see that the man had speeded up his pace as well.

She wished she had waited for the all night bus, but seeing she had half an hour to wait, knew she could be home in that time.

Seeing no one else around except cars traveling fast in the rain, she started to run, feeling sure the man was a mugger, or worse still, the 2 a.m. killer.

"Just another hundred yards or so and I'll be home." She thought, as she ran as fast as she could.

Seconds later she felt a tug on her shoulder and gave a piercing scream as a cut throat razor cut into her neck; she lowered her head and bit deep into the hand holding the razor.

The man dropped the razor swearing, and punched the woman's head.

As he bent down to pick up the razor, he heard footsteps running towards him and a loud police whistle being blown, leaving the razor, he turned to run round the back of a block of flats to make his escape.

The police officer stayed with the woman after calling for back up and picked up the cutthroat razor, then phoned for an ambulance.

Shortly, two response cars pulled up with six armed officers who jumped out and ran in the direction the assailant had gone.

Overhead a police helicopter had arrived, and its strong searchlight soon picked out the wanted man and in a few minutes he was taken prisoner and whisked off to New Scotland Yard for questioning.

The woman who had been attacked was taken to ST. Thomas's hospital for medical attention and fortunately, only needed a few stitches in her neck and was able to speak clearly.

D.C.I. Dean and his sergeant went straight to the hospital to talk to the woman first hand, and she was able go into some detail.

They noted her name was Mrs. Jane Masters, an office cleaner, who told them how she left work and decided to walk home, when she heard the man behind her she became scared, and the police know the rest, she then told them he was over six feet tall, heavily built, clean shaven and smelt of alcohol, and she thinks she would pick him out in a line up.

Desmond Dean was elated, "Sergeant Osborn, we've got our man," he said, "We'll go to the yard and do our own interview, this will look good on my record," then add, "And on yours of course!"

I hope your right sir," said Roger, "But it does seem to me unlike the way he has done other killings."

"Nonsense sergeant, it's him all right, let's get to the Yard!"

Once in the interview room D.C.I. Dean looked over his notes and said, "Your name is Stanley Shaw, and this interview is being taped, anything you say may be taken down and used in evidence, do you understand that? And remember we have your cutthroat razor!"

"Yes I know it's being taped," came the reply, "I am your 2.a.m. killer, and I sure gave you all the run a round," he said laughing, "I admit I tried to kill that woman tonight, and I would have done if you lot hadn't turned up, the same as I sliced all the others, but women, they are all the same, when I was a kid my mother used to beat be with a stick, the old bag was always drunk, and I had so many different 'uncles' and no father that I knew of, so to me they are all the same."

"Why kill the Northern M.P?" asked Dean.

"She's a woman aint she?" came the grinning reply.

Roger Osborn then asked, Why did you kill blind Ted? he did you no harm."

"Cos' I wanted to, that's why!"
he answered, "Gimee a fag,"

"What about the others?" said Roger, "And describe the inside of Sir Roland Squires flat."

"Gimee a fag first, I know my rights, and then I'll tell yer all about 'is place." came the reply.

Roger Osborn stood up and said, "You are wasting police time, there is no such person as Sir Roland Squires, and you are not the person responsible for the murders that have taken place, but you will be charged with the attempted murder of the woman you almost killed and for wasting police time."

He beckoned an officer to take him to the cells were he would be kept on remand until a suitable date for a court appearance would be arranged.

Roger looked at his D.C.I. and said, "Well sir, let's hope it won't be too long before we get the break we want and find the real killer, but it is possible that he may have killed the Immigrant woman near the dome, as the doctor said the killer may well be left handed and our man in there is!"

"I sincerely hope you are right on that sergeant, It would be a feather in our caps if that is so, but if they bring in officers from other parts of the country, I won't be held responsible for future developments that turn out to be wrong will I?" said his D.C.I.

Roger Osborn just nodded in reply and said, "We can sleep on it sir, even if we only have a few hours left right now, and I am ready for bed!"

Chapter 8

Don Grant was staying at Jack Farley's flat, declining the hospitality flat he was offered at New Scotland Yard.

Opening the morning paper that was always promptly delivered by seven o'clock he called out to Jack.

"Hey old buddy, it says here that that Perez guy your boys captured the other day seems to have skipped bail, he has missed the last two bail appearances at your Bond Street police station that he was supposed to be at by ten o'clock in the morning, the guy that let him out on bail must have a screw loose, even on a half million pound of your money, hell man, he will get that back in no time in a dozen different ways!"

"What did you say?" said Jack, "Read that bit out loud again,"

Don did so, and Jack exploded, saying, "When the Ravenhill gang and the Cooper brothers find out he's skipped bail there will be all hell to pay; we get some stupid idiot in a gown sitting on a bench, and thinks because he is not affected it will do no harm to give Perez a large bail amount that will keep him in tow, hell Don, Perez wouldn't even miss it, he's a vicious killer that probably mugged his own grandmother!"

Don smiled slyly and said, "What say you and me go get him old buddy, like the time we had in Hawaii?"

"Now that sounds o.k. by me pal," said Jack, "The most they can do is sack me and send you back to Uncle Sam! but first I must phone my mate Alex, and see if his nark can tell us where Perez is hiding out now."

Ten minutes later Jack said, "He's come up trumps again Don, I don't know how he does it just being in the stores, but he's the man to see when you're not sure which way to turn, but he said Perez is holed up in the old Battersea Power Station with just a handful of his old team, so to use your words Don, let's go old buddy."

Leaving their car some distance away,

they saw some minor repair work being done near the main gates so they headed there.

The two men knew they would be easy targets for Perez going in as they were, so they knew just what to do.

Jack showed his Met police warrant card to the four workers and said, "This is police business, you must leave the area immediately."

They then borrowed two of their donkey jackets and hard hats and went in through the main gates, making as if they were checking the structure of parts of the dilapidated building and at the same time keeping a close watch higher up, knowing that would be the obvious choice for Perez to be, although he would have positioned his few gang members at various places to use as vantage points just in case they had been followed.

Seeing a slight movement near an old broken door, Jack put on an Irish accent and said, "Begorrah now Pat, 'tis either a rat movin' about or someone I see dossin' down over there for the night so it is, tis' a cold mornin' so if it's an old tramp I'll leave him so I will, oi've been in the same position me self so I have many a time."

Some thirty yards further on two men emerged from a doorway and walked towards the two detectives.

The first one spoke in fairly good english and said, "What are you two doing here? we are prospective buyers and were not told work was being done here, go back where you came from now and leave us to do our own surveying."

"Well now sir, "said Jack, "oi might be askin' the same as you now so oi will, but oi'II do better than that sir so I will, oi'll mobile me boss so oi will."

As Jack made as if to get his mobile phone out the gangster said, "No need to phone…" and the pair were shocked to see revolvers in the hands of the two detectives in place of mobile phones.

"Inside quickly," said Jack pointing at the doorway the two men had just came from, "One false move and your dead, try going for your guns and I'll drop you

were you stand and my friend will be happy to do the same, we came here looking for Perez, so take us to him."
The pock marked gangster looked at Jack and said, "Youa cama to seea Marco Perez before, I recognise youa nowa."
"That's me buddy boy," said Jack, "Now move or you've eaten your last bowl of spaghetti!"
The two gangsters wavered for a few moments then turned towards the opening.
In a flash the pock marked crook spun round and went for his gun.
"Tut-tut," said Jack as he fired one shot and hit the gangster between the eyes, who was dead before he hit the ground.
"You heard my friend," said Don Grant, "Move, or you will join your friend, "Take us to Perez now."
At that moment two shots rang out from different parts of the buildings, neither scored a hit, as the two men and their prisoner moved inside, checking that there were no other gang members waiting for them.

Jack grabbed the frightened man and said, "Where's Perez hiding? lie to me and your dead meat, speak now, and say how many of your crowd here?"

"He's on the other side of the building, up two floors, near the flag pole you can see from here, he has six men with him, don't shoot me please!"

"Handcuff him to the railings Don, I'll mobile the yard and tell them were we are, they won't be very happy, but if we bring in Perez, that will satisfy them for a while, so if we jump in that J.C,B, digger they can't hit us," then laughed as he said, "Well it works in the movies!"

The two men ran to the large J.C.B. digger and raised the large scoop so that their position was out of sight, switching on the engine, the huge machine slowly made its way across the open space to the part of the building where Perez was hiding.

A couple of shots came from behind them that made no impression, so Don Grant eyed his man up and fired one shot and saw the gangster collapse in a heap.

"One less to worry about old buddy."
he said to Jack, who was at the controls.
"Nicely done Don." he replied.
At that moment a burst of an automatic
gun shattered part of the windscreen. Jack
said, "That's a Kalashnikov without a
doubt, keep your head down Don,
anyway the heavy gang sent here from
the yard should be here soon, they are
based only about ten minutes away."
Moments later the police sirens could be
heard and three motor vans screeched
into the power station.
Their highly trained officers jumped clear
and took up defensive positions as the
officer in charge called though a loud
hailer, "Come out with your hands high
and throw your weapons in front of you,
then lay down flat with your arms out
stretched, you have no escape and you
have two minutes to make up your minds,
if not, we will come in and get you, fire
one shot at us, and we will return your
fire. Your time starts now!"
Inside the two minutes, the remaining
gangsters came out, lastly Marco Perez

who looked at Jack Farley with hatred in his eyes as Jack jumped down from the digger and kicked the gang leader's weapon out of reach saying, "I hope they send you back home soon Perez, because over there, all the money you have stashed away won't help you at all, and for you it will be the chop, I just wish you had shown yourself earlier to me, I would have finished you off in the same way as I would have squashed a maggot, I am not a do gooder and never have been, I've always wanted the punishment to fit the crime, and it's payback time now for all the people you've had killed or injured, I hope you rot in hell!"

With that, Jack turned and walked away, leaving him and his gang members to the elite squad.

Back at New Scotland Yard the two men received a dressing down from the commissioner to start with, who then told them, "This is not 'The gunfight at the o.k. corral,' although the press might well think so, in future you will only use any firearm when you have direct permission from an authorised officer, if you are unsure, call in first."

Then added, "Unofficially I thank you for that, as bringing in Perez has stopped what could have been a nasty situation with gang warfare on the streets,

I know you won't tell me how you knew where to go, just do your reports when you leave this office, and in future, leave your weapons in the armoury, apart from that carry on with your normal duties."

Don Grant asked if he could stay with Jack, and was told. "Yes, providing they did not take the law into their own hands again, if so, he would be on the next plane back to America."

They were then given the rest of the day off, but to be on call if needed.

The later afternoon editions of the newspapers made it out to be just as the Commissioner had guessed.

One paper had headlines, "Gun fight at The O.K. Corral," (but in this case, Battersea Power Station.) Another said. "Shootout in the City, Gangsters blasted to death in dramatic swoop by special

police."
Jack laughed and said, "Don mate,
the people that do the wording on these
papers should be film script writers."
Don Grant shook his head as he said,
"It's an everyday occurrence in New
York Jack, and most any town in
America, you're lucky if you get two
days without getting your gun out, but
over here there are so many restrictions as
to who can wear a gun, and who can't,
and you must not shoot unless given the
o.k. hey man, when your life's on the line
you sure as hell don't wait for someone to
play god and let him decide to let the
other guy shoot first, If that had happened
to me even once state side, wouldn't be
here now!"
"I know what you mean," Jack replied,
"But over here it's a different ball game,
some of our rules are rubbish and some
are good, at times some are bent a little
and some are broken, like you we have
good cops and bent cops, so if every one
of ours were armed, a lot of innocent
people would be injured or killed,

besides, you have licenced gun shops everywhere in America, how many innocent people get killed because of that? I wouldn't want that here Don; it's bad enough as it is but I guess we all do the best we can."

Over the next week nothing happened out of the ordinary and Nick and Candy were practically finalised with their wedding plans.

Jack was to be their best man, Emma will be the chief bridesmaid and they had booked an open carriage and will have a police escort and they had planned their honeymoon at a Butlin's holiday camp!

Reporting for duty the following morning Jack was surprised to find his old mentor Alex Ford was not at the stores, or his 'listening post' as he called it.

A young constable was in the stores office as Jack and Don walked in and said, "Good morning sir, can I help you?"

"I hope so constable," said Jack, "Where is Alex this morning? I've never known him to be late or be off sick for that matter, is he O.K.?"

The constable said, "He is in sir, right now in the commissioner's office, he has had some very sad news, but I am not at liberty to discuss it with anyone right now."

"What do you mean by very sad news son?" Replied Jack, "Alex and I go back a long way, I am sure he won't mind you telling me the problem."

At that moment Alex appeared in the doorway in civilian clothes and said to the constable, "You can go now son, but come back in twenty minutes and you will be in charge of the stores for the next couple of weeks, thank you."

The young constable nodded and left the office.

Jack looked at his old friend and could see the pained look on his face and said, "Alex mate, whatever is the trouble? maybe we can help in some way, don't bottle it up, and are you ill with something you're not telling us? and why the civvy clothes, and off work for two or three weeks? It's not a serious illness is it?"

Alex looked up said, "The 2 a.m. killer has struck again Jack, only this time it was Judy, my ex-wife, we had our differences I know Jack, but I still loved her, and if ever she needed help she knew she only had to ask."

Tears streamed down his face as he spoke, Jack was lost for words seeing his old friend in such a state.

"Where abouts did it happen Alex? and where was Judy at the time?" Jack asked his old friend.

Alex straightened himself up and said, "She phoned me around 1.40 a.m. this morning, I was asleep at the time and it was the phone ringing that woke me up, as you know Judy remarried after we were divorced and although she was happy at first, it did not stay that way for very long, and it was not a happy marriage by all accounts as they split up a couple of times, although Judy did try to make a go of it, but he was a womaniser and gambled most of her money away, when he lost it all he made out he had changed and wanted her back to try again, this time it seems Judy had had enough of his lies and the phone call to me was to ask if she could stay with me for a few days while she sorted things out, I said certainly she could and I would be with her inside half an hour by Westminster underground station, when I got there I saw small crowd of people that must have been to a late night show or something, and a police constable talking to them, my heart skipped a few beats as I thought of the 2a.m. killer in the area.

I pulled up by the kerb and rushed over hoping I was wrong and just at that time D.C.I. Dean and sergeant Roger Osborn arrived, Jack mate, it was my Judy lying there with her throat cut open and that Inspector Dean is not worth a candle, he looked at sergeant Osborn and said, 'it looks like we have another one,' I said to him, that's my wife you're talking about inspector, I'm not a violent man, but I won't hold myself responsible for my actions if you don't treat her with respect."

Sergeant Osborn stepped in and said.

"It's just his way Alex, it's nothing personal."

"Then I identified the body and one of the officers used my car and drove me home."

Jack sat Alex down and offered him a cigarette, then smiled as he said.

"I remember now, you always smoked cheroots, sorry mate I don't smoke them myself."

Alex lit one of his own and said.

"I've been thinking Jack, do you think that Judy's husband could be the killer? His name is Mike Moore, he stays out late at night in gambling clubs in this area, he is a very tall man and gets violent at times by all accounts, and likes his drink, should it turn out it is him, I will make a promise to Judy that I will kill him myself and I would not try to cover up what I've done!"

Jack looked at him and said. "Slow down Alex, if it is him, he will be checked out properly and there is no way he will get away with it, you know that yourself, what with D.N.A. tests, and a search of his premises, if he is guilty they will certainly find something useful and incriminating there, you know that most of that type of murderers like to keep a souvenir of what they have done, I'll tell you something in secret mate, but you must keep it to yourself and not tell a soul, O.k.?"

Alex gave a half grin and said, "Jack boy, you know me better than that, in fact you know me better than anyone, you have my word on it."

Jack smiled and said, "Sorry mate, of course I know! well the only other people that know are The Commissioner, the Chief Superintendent, Roger Osborn and Don Grant, The truth is I am still on the 2 a.m. murders Case, I've never been off it, the traffic duties job was a put on as it seems there may be a mole in here somewhere, and I am getting closer than before, somewhere in the back of my mind is the answer and it will re-surface before long mate, of that I am sure."

Alex gave a short laugh and said, "You fooled me at first Jack, but when you and your mate got Marco Perez in a gun fight, I had heard not so much as a squeak that you was still on the case, but I knew that it was not the work of someone on traffic duties, and I am glad you've still got your finger in the pie so to speak! please check out Judy's husband and if he is two detectives spent hours sifting through the dozens of witnesses' the one we want, let me be the first to know!"

Back in a spare room Jack had been allocated, the statements, police statements, notes connected with the different murders and anything that might throw some light on things that may prove helpful in some way to solve the mystery, all it proved was that they were looking at a loner who knew London well, an educated person with some influence in police or government work, possibly a civil servant or even someone working in any number of departments in the Houses of Parliament, most of it fruitless with very little to show for it.

 Jack looked at Don and said, "It's quite possible that a member of parliament or two might be holding back on us Don for some reason or other, so we will head over that way and ruffle a few feathers."

Chapter 9

At Westminster the two detectives were allocated a room where any of the members, either men or women could speak to them in the strictest of confidence, in that whatever was said would not be repeated outside of the room they were in except to the commissioner of police at Scotland Yard regardless of their political beliefs.

At first is seemed that no one was interested, then when they were reassured again by Jack that it was for their own safety, one by one they waited in line to see them.

Firstly Jack asked them if they had noticed anyone following them when they were not in Westminster, or seeing the same person in restaurants, bars or train journeys who seemed to be looking in their direction a lot.

Most of them appeared worried after the northern Member of Parliament was killed unexpectedly and asked for police protection, although Jack could not promise that unless they had been threatened, or had a stalker following their movements.

A number of gay M.P.'s were very concerned that they may be targeted, both men and women, and Jack told them they would do what they could when they made their report to the commissioner, and then asked if any had taken up the offer of protection by the Hooper's or the Ravenhill's, if so, it would be just a mention in their reports at the Yard!

Jack said to each of them, "They are both very good at what they do in that respect, just as safe as the S.A.S. and although it is frowned on by the establishment, that part of their set up is quite legal, and if you think their rates are steep, imagine having just a routine check every hour by the police, or twenty four hour protection by them until the killer is caught, the choice is yours, I am not trying to sway you one way or the other, just giving you the facts, maybe nothing will happen, I hope that is so, but the bottom line is, it is down to you!"

That evening Jack and Don called to check on Sylvia and Emma who ran to both of them and gave them a big hug. Sylvia had made them a large apple pie to take back with them, and then settled them in for a tea time treat.

After they had been assured that everything was fine with Sylvia and Emma, who had gotten over being kidnapped knowing that Jack had arranged a reputable security firm to keep watch on them both until the case was closed made them all feel secure in that area. Emma sat on Jack's lap and said, "Uncle Jack and you Don, I've got to talk to you both very seriously about you both giving up smoking! I've told mum she has to stop for her own health and mine, and she has not had a ciggie for two days now and I am very proud of her."

Jack looked at Don and said, "Don mate, I've been smoking for years, probably since I was about fourteen years old, how about you?"

Don blinked a couple of times and said, "My old grand pappy smoked an old pipe he made himself when I was around ten years old, and I used to ask him to let me have a puff, then he would laugh when I had a coughing fit after I tried it, so he used to roll a ciggie for me once in a while and used to say, "Don't tell your mam or daddy or they will lynch me! so that was our secret, but I think they knew and let me carry on, so that is a lot of smoking years young lady, and now I smoke cigars, so it won't be easy to stop now!"

Emma looked at him and frowned before saying, "Between us we will get there Don, but you must try hard and don't give in, I know it won't be easy for you, but mum is trying as well, and so will uncle Jack if I have my way, I don't mind if he has patches, and I know you Americans like to chew gum, so you can do it that way, but give it a go please, it will benefit all of us in the long run, so I think it is reasonable if you both have your last smoke today, then ditch any you have left last thing tonight."

Then looking up at them she gave a beaming smile and said. "As the yanks say, put it there pal, shake on it!" Both the detectives tried not to laugh, but realised that Emma meant what she said as she held out her hand to shake on it.

Jack spoke first saying, "Emma darling, it's not that easy to stop smoking straight away, especially when the kind of work we do is stressful at times, and sometimes we need a smoke to steady our nerves after a hard day, suppose we say that when this case is over we will give it our best shot, how does that sound to you.?" Emma smiled and said, "That's fine by me."

And both men took her little hand and said, "Cubs honour Emma, you've got a deal!"

Don looked at Emma and said, "When I was in college in New York State I learnt how to do a lot of magic tricks in my spare time, well I called them magic anyway! Would you like to see some of them now?"

"Yes please Don," Emma said," Mummy and me watch those programmes on the tele and try to see how they are done, most of the time we don't know though, they are very clever, and I would love to see you on the tele and I would tell all my friends at school to look out for you as you are a friend of my uncle Jack's."

"Don grinned at Jack and said to him, "Lend me a ten pound note please Jack, you sign your name on it first, then I will put it in an envelope and mix it up with two more, then you tell me what two to burn, and hope you chose the right one to keep!"

Sylvia, Emma and Jack watched closely as Don mixed the three envelopes very quickly and then laid them on the table saying to Jack, "Tell me what two to burn Jack, remember, it's your money."

I think my money is safe Don," Jack said, as he pushed two envelopes forward for Don to burn in a metal bowl.

"Are you sure it's those two I can burn Jack?" Don replied. "Yes mate those two." said Jack.

"Emma squealed with laughter when Jack opened the remaining envelope and found it to be empty.

And she said, "Uncle Jack, you told Don what two envelopes to burn."

But Jack said, "Emma, I was going to give the ten pound note to you after Don had done the trick!"

Don said, "Hang on a second Emma, what's that behind your ear?"

He leaned forward, and from behind her ear he took the ten pound note with Jack's name on it and gave it to her and said, "Now that's magic!"

And for the next hour he kept them entertained and baffled with different card tricks and making handkerchiefs change colour and all kind of coin tricks, even Jack was unable to see how most of them were done.

Later on it was time for them to go, but the two detectives first checked the security officer was on duty and then said their goodbyes to Sylvia and Emma, promising to call on them again during the week and phone them at different times of the day to make sure everything was fine.

"That Little Emma sure is one fine young lady," said Don, "When she gets married I'd bet my last dollar that she will wear the trousers in their house!"

Jack grinned and said. "You've got to be right on that pal."

The following day the American was assigned to an accident unit that patrolled the major motor ways for any emergencies that often happened, and he could see that it was no different here than it was in the states with people taking chances and reckless driving. Although he was just an observer he was able to assist in helping the paramedics when needed, and re-directing traffic.

Meanwhile Jack Farley continued sifting through what little evidence there was, as what witness's statements there were, mostly conflicted with each other.

Another visit to Blind Ted's flat that was still cordoned off in case there may be a clue of any kind that will help.

As he expected, no one on the estate had seen anything out of place that day, and Jack knew even if someone had seen anything out of the ordinary, they would keep shtum and say nothing.

But he still had this nagging thought that he had forgotten a missing piece to the jigsaw puzzle, and if he could just remember what it was, it would fall into place.

He had just left his favourite fish and chip restaurant and was walking back to his car, still pondering over the missing piece of the puzzle when his sixth sense alerted him of danger, but as he half turned and moved his head to one side, a crashing blow hit him on the side of his head and he felt himself falling to the ground in what appeared to be slow motion.

He heard running footsteps, and more distant voices saying, "Someone call an ambulance, he is bleeding from the head, I noticed him walking a bit in front of me and my mate, and then someone rushed out of a side turning and hit him on the head with something, it might have been

a mugger who saw me and ran off!"
And another saying. "I think he is dead,
there's blood everywhere!"
He wanted to say, "I can hear you, I am
awake, can't you see that?"
But no speech came as he drifted into a
state of semi-conciseness and in what
seemed like a film to him, he was able to
see himself as a teenager again with all
his old friends he knew and other people
from those far off days of his youth.
Lads he had played conkers with and
played tag in the school playground
chasing each other, and the odd
schoolroom romance that never amounted
to anything more than a quick kiss.
All these things flashed through his mind
in an instant, but what seemed ages to
himself.
In the next scene he was older and had
become friends with a boy called Ron
Ravenhill who flouted authority, and
always seemed to do his own thing and
no one ever picked on.
Even though Jack's dad was a policeman
their friendship grew, both in their

schooldays and afterwards.

But by this time Ron Ravenhill was beginning to make a name for himself, both as a wide boy and someone that you did not upset, both to the police who pulled him in now and then on petty crimes that he just got a warning for.

And one or two older villains' that saw he would be an asset to their gang as an enforcer to start with, then work his way up through their ranks, as he was a boy that had no time for authority unless it suited him and he would not crack under pressure.

Also he had most of the teenage gangs and would-be tearaways living in Dagenham where he lived scared of him as he would use fists, bike chains and anything that he could get hold of, if anyone thought they could take him on, and he never lost a fight!

He was a good looking lad that had the local girls playing up to him, but his ambition was to become the top man of his own gang, something he did after his army national service that came to a sudden halt!

He had a sister called Lola who could fight almost as hard as Ron and was like a tigress when upset!

Although he was a hard nut, Ron was a sucker for the underdog, and often went out of his way to do a good turn for any deserving cause, mostly without the person knowing who their benefactor was, he would not have bullying in his 'employment' as he called it, and if anyone did try it on, they would answer to him.

As schoolboys they were great friends, and even though Jack's father was a policeman, that did not stop young Ron from swiping apples and pears off of market traders stalls, or climbing into empty houses to take anything left behind that he could sell himself.

On the sports field he was very competitive, even at football he would trip up the opposition to score a goal or two, and was often sent off for foul play, but Ron would just laugh it off and say, "If you don't like the heat, stay out of the kitchen!"

Even in the Jack's state of semi-consciousness he was able to re-live his young man days. Again he drifted back to the times they would play snooker for hours on end in the large hall above Burton's stores that were in most towns or at the Y.M.C.A. then in the pubs when they were of age.

Jack's dad did not like him going into pubs, but Jack assured him he only drank orange juice, which was true!

After a while both lads went their different ways, Jack joined the police force as a cadet, while Ron became part of one of the bigger gangs in the area.

Chapter 10

Although Jack could still see his past days as if he was watching a film, he could faintly hear an ambulance coming his way with its sirens blaring but once again he drifted off as if in a dream…

He saw himself struggling with a giant of a lad about his own age, trying to stop him battering another youth beside a motor cycle, the big lad spun round and threw a punch that almost closed Jack's eye.

He staggered back but came forward again, ducking under the big lads swinging fists, and using his police unarmed combat training, he pushed the other lad's arm up his back causing him to shout out, "Let go of my bleedin' arm, that's my Norton motorbike he's trying to nick!"

"Calm down mate and stop struggling, other police officers will get him." Jack said.

"I don't care if you're the bleedin' foreign legion," The lad said, "I fight my own battles, and I'll break every bone in his body for trying to nick my bike, so let me go or I'll bust you in half too!"

It took several police officers to subdue him before taking both of them to the Walthamstow police station where Jack had been posted for the day.

The youth that owned the motor cycle's name was Bert Hooper, he well known to the local police as was his brother Bill.

Mainly because Bert was one of the youngest cage fighters on the circuit, just seventeen years old and about six feet six inches tall, weighing in at almost fourteen stone.

He started cage fighting at sixteen, as he had seen big money change hands before and after a fight.

Although he was up against experienced fighters and got many cuts and bruises, he learned fast and trained hard and was more than a match for any novice cage fighter he fought.

He often made the sporting pages, both in photos and fight reports. And was popular with the heavy gang that promoted many of his fights.

The big shot villain that ruled the roost in those days was an ex- professional light-heavy weight boxer called Johnny (No Mercy) Chapman; he had fought for the British championship but lost only on badly cut eyes.

He was given that ring name as he fought like an animal in the ring (and out of it) he trained at the Fitzroy Gym in London, always known as 'The Jungle' and he was the man that made sure Bert was always in tip top condition.

Bert was nobody's fool and as well as talent, he had brains and brawn, and made sure he was well paid to get in the ring and fight.

His twin brother Bill was unpredictable and had a violent temper, he was almost as tall as Bert, and was often in trouble with the police and had spent a few nights in the cells when he got drunk.

It was mainly Bert who could control him when he got upset, because Bert could see they could be on a nice little earner if they played their cards right.

He knew that No Mercy had made enough money to retire to Spain where many crooks finished up, and that he was a crook through and through, and had heard he had organised a raid on a gold bullion train at one time and got away with millions of pounds in gold blocks, he and two others got away, but three others were caught, and ended up in prison.

The police still wanted him for questioning over the robbery, but so far he had evaded capture.

Bert had made up his mind that when his two years army service was over, by then Johnny Chapman would be living it up in Spain or doing a stretch in the slammer! And the way would be clear for the Hooper twins to take over!

But he knew 'No Mercy' owned three or four cafes where quite a lot of drug dealing was done and as big as he was, he knew no one stepped out of line where Johnny Chapman was concerned.

But by then Bert and Bill would be the kingpins of that area.

Bill Hooper did get his call up papers, but was doing Ha term in prison for grievous bodily harm, and although the national service would not have accepted him, he would not have lasted long with service authority anyway.

Bert was called up and joined the Essex regiment along with another would- be gangster, Ron Ravenhill, who between them soon found they could rob the stores easily and sell clothes, blankets, boots etc., before they were transferred to Korea where they done their own thing once the war was over, until Ron Ravenhill had an argument with a bolshie officer who he grabbed hold of, and threatened to throw him over the mountainside…

Jack was trying to gain full consciousness and could hear someone saying, "Here come the Para-medics now."

But he lapsed once again back into his young life…In the charge room at Walthamstow police station Jack Farley explained to the duty sergeant what he saw, and how he was given a black eye by Hooper while attempting to stop him belting a youth who was bending over a motor cycle.

It transpires that the motor cycle was indeed Bert Hooper's and the other person was about to steal it and ride away when Bert caught him in the act.

The desk sergeant was an avid cage fighting fan and had seen many of Bert's fights.

So he said, "Mister Hooper had every right to stop the would be thief attempting to steal his motor cycle, also he did not know you are a police cadet, that is something you should have told him immediately, and I am sure most public spirited people would have done exactly the same thing in mister Hooper's position as you most probably would have done yourself, bring the accused here it is not the first time he has been nicked, his name is Sid Jackson and he knows the inside of our cells just as much as our officers! and he will be charged with an attempted felony."

Looking at Bert the desk sergeant said,

"When is your next fight Bert?"

"Next Saturday night sarge, it should be a belter" he replied.

And winked as he said. "I'll leave your two tickets behind the bar at the Rose and Crown pub, like always!"

The sergeant gave a slight cough, and nodded as Bert walked away.

Over the next few month's Jack had a few ups and downs with the Hooper twins, and although Bill was short tempered, Bert kept him under control and Jack found them to be likable rouges, mostly one step ahead of the law, but what Jack would call 'good Baddies' and he became good friends with Bert Hooper.

As the medics lifted him into the ambulance, Jack gave a groan and tried to shake his head.

One of the medics said to his colleague, "We've not lost him Paul, he is trying to come round, and the hospital is only ten minutes away, so let's get a move on!"

The ambulance driver put his foot down

and they were at the hospital in seven minutes flat.

In no time they had rushed Jack to the operating theatre where he stayed for the next forty-five minutes during a delicate operation.

Even under the anaesthetic his mind still played funny tricks.

He recalled going fishing with his dad and how he would laugh if he caught a big fish and his dad got only a small one or none at all, and his mum would say, "Your better at fishing Jack, your dad nods off to sleep and forgets the fish just eat his bait then swim away."

He saw himself on his passing out parade at Hendon watched by his proud mum and dad, and when he was awarded a certificate for the best recruit of the intake, he could see again the tears of happiness running down his mum's face, and watching the way that his dad hugged him and shook his hand as if it was really happening again right now.

And the sadness in his heart at his dad's funeral, after he was on traffic duty and was run down and killed by a hit and run driver who was eventually caught.

And smiled in satisfaction, remembering how he exacted retribution in his own way after the driver got a laughable sentence and a small fine, he thought of the words in the bible, "Vengeance is mine sayeth the lord."

And said to himself, "That evens the score up dad!"

And how his mother had died shortly afterwards by what was called 'natural causes,' although he knew it was really a broken heart.

Somewhere through what seemed like a mist, he could hear his father talking to him saying. "Go back son, your time is not now, you have much to live for and so much more to do, your friends are praying and waiting for you to revive, we will be here when your time on earth is over, but go back now."

The words trailed off as Jack opened his eyes and the nurse at his bedside called out, "The patient has opened his eyes, he is trying to speak!"

A doctor hurried in and confirmed that his breathing, heart rate and pulse were all normal and said, "He is a very strong man, with rest he will survive, after five minutes or so he can have visitors."

Chapter 11

Waiting to go in were Nick Stone and Don Grant, they looked at Jack propped up in bed with his head swathed in bandages and Nick said, "Bloody hell guv. I can't leave you on your own for long without you getting lumbered! you got shot in the arm in Miami when I left you on your own for a while, and now we find out someone's belted you on the head and you end up in a hospital bed, but seriously Jack, have you any idea who done it?"

"No I haven't Nick, at the last moment I sensed someone was behind me and I started to turn, then bingo, that was all remember until now."

He then told them of the flashbacks to his younger days, and how his dad had told him his time to go was not yet, as he still had work to do in this world.

Don told him that there were two witnesses who saw what happened but were unable to catch the assailant as he went quickly down a side ally, and being dark they had no chance of catching him. Their descriptions of him appeared to match the sketchy ones they had of the 2.a.m. killer, and it seemed that Jack was being targeted again by the unknown assailant.

Jack looked weary, so the two men left him to rest just as his old mentor Alex Ford rushed in to the ward.

"Can I see him for a few minutes?" he asked, He looked so upset and concerned that the doctor said. "Yes, but five minutes only!"

Alex thanked him and sat beside his old friend, he gave his hand a squeeze and said, "I'll get the bastard that done this to you Jack, if it's the last thing I do, I looked upon you as the son I never had when you were my rookie copper, I know your dad was always so very proud of you, anyway I'm going to get back like it used to be when we were on the beat together, I just hope he picks on me even at my age Jack mate, I'll be ready for him, although I've still got strong doubts about my ex-wife's husband, he's out and about and no one has bothered to question him yet."

Jack was half asleep as the doctor came and said. "You'll have to go now sir, Mister Farley needs a lot of rest now."

Alex stood up and said. "Thank you for letting me see him so soon doctor, I will phone in tomorrow to check how he is if I may, thank you again."

Nick and Don waited for Alex then drove him back to New Scotland Yard.

On the way there, Alex told them of how Jack Farley first started out with him as his mentor.

He was about twenty years older than Jack and had been in the police force all his adult life, starting out as a cadet like Jack, and working his way up to a sergeant before reaching retirement age.

The force had been his life, so when he was offered a post as store man at New Scotland Yard he jumped at it and had been there ever since.

When he got married he wanted a son that could follow on in his footsteps, his wife Judy said, "Wait a couple of years, then we can start a family."

Six months passed, and he told them how Judy had complained that he was hardly ever at home because he was always volunteering for one thing or another, and at times was away three or four days a week, so she refused to become pregnant unless he spent more time at home.

He told them they often rowed about it, and although he loved her dearly he always put the job first, then one day she told him if he put the job before her she would leave him.

He said he knew he had a temper when roused but had always kept it under control.

Then he continued telling the two men, "I don't know why, but I slapped her round the face and made her mouth bleed, I'm six foot three and fourteen stone, I never should have done it I know, and it is something I've always regretted doing, so she packed a few things in a bag and walked out on me, I begged her to stay, but she said that although she still loved me, she could no longer trust me not to get violent again, we could stay friends but no more than that, I was truly devastated and could see that she meant it, so when Jack came on the scene, there was the son I had always wanted."

Nick and Don listened to all Alex had told them and could tell that he was pleased to tell strangers, as he was more open knowing they would not spread around what he had told them.

He said to Nick, "Make sure you don't let the job ruin your marriage Nick, like it did mine even promotion is no guarantee that it will be foreverness, keep you free time away from the force, look at me now, I'm just a lonely old man in the stores that helps out now and then!"

"Don't be so hard on yourself Alex," Nick said to him, "You are well respected by everyone, from the top brass down, you run things like clockwork and whoever takes your place will have a very hard act to follow."

Don said. "Hey Alex, you were saying at first about your rookie Jack Farley, this I gotta hear!"

Alex grinned as he said, "Well I knew he had swotted up on all aspects of the law and his old dad made sure of that, but at times he frustrated both his dad and me by bending the rules more than just a little bit, how he got away with some of his strokes I will never know, sometimes I was able to cover up his way of working things, and other times he was called into Superintendent's office for a right bollocking, but it was like water off a ducks back to him, he had always wanted to join the C.I.D, that's the criminal investigation department Don, rather like your F.B.I. he said there was more scope in that type of investigating police work than a uniformed copper as it meant dealing with the real villains out there, and I suppose he was right in saying that because he was cut out for that line of work. He was always smartly dressed, unlike a lot of other constables' and made many friends on the beat giving a big smile and a friendly wave to most of the shopkeepers and passers- by, when the time came for him to be transferred to the

C.I.D. I was sorry to lose him, but I could see his future was in the plain cloths branch."

They pulled up at the Yard, and Alex told them any time they wanted a chat he would be in the stores except in the evenings where he would be patrolling in the red light district hoping to meet 'public enemy number one' as he called it.

As Alex got out of the car, Nick shook his head saying, "Don't leave yourself open for that Alex, you of all people know extra police are on the lookout for him night and day now, and sooner or later we will catch him."

Alex gave a rueful grin and said. "I've no one else left in this world Nick, if I die catching him it will be worthwhile as Jack is my friend, but I thank you for your concern."

And with that remark turned and walked away.

The following day Sylvia was at the hospital and as soon as she was allowed in she was at Jack's bedside.

"Jack darling," She said taking his hand, "Nick phoned and told me you were in hospital and it was such a shock, at first I wondered what had happened till he told me you had been hit on the head from behind, you must be more careful when you go it alone, it seems the killer knows you, but you don't know him."

Jack smiled at her and said, "It's a good job he hit me on the head Sylvia, you know the old saying, 'No sense, no feeling,' but seeing you here makes me feel so much better and I am not going to stay here in this hospital any longer than I have to, I don't mind coming back for check-ups, but that's all."

His face hardened as he became 'Jack Farley, policeman' once again.

Sylvia said, "You're a stubborn old fool Jack Farley, you never give up do you? the doctor said you will be in here about a week and need to rest, if you want to come home with me I will be your nurse! but you must rest.

"Sylvia you're an old fusspot and I love you for it, but I just want to get back to work again, Don will be with me for as long as he is in England so I won't be alone, I promise I won't start back for a week, but I just want to get up and out of here as soon as possible, tomorrow if I can swing it with the doctor!"

Sylvia looked hard at him and said, "Why must you be so pig headed Jack? but I know you will never change so I will go along with it, but if you feel you need a nursemaid or a rest you must promise to come and stay with Emma and me, o.k.?"

Jack grinned and said, "I like it when you get angry Sylvia, sure thing, that's a promise."

Chapter 12

The following day Jack was listening to the early morning radio news, when he heard the news reader say. "New Scotland Yard announced early this morning that a police constable on duty last night came across the body of a woman who they believe maybe the six or seventh victim of who the press call the 2 a.m. killer on the embankment near Lambeth Bridge, the victim, who has not yet been named has had her throat cut similar to the other victims.

She is described as white, in her mid-thirties and may well come from the Lambeth area, we will broadcast any news flashes as, and when they come through."

Jack turned the radio off and asked to speak to the duty doctor.

He said. "I thank you, and all your hard working staff for the utmost care and attention you have shown me during, and after my operation I could not have asked for more, but I am discharging myself as now. The doctor said in a surprised tone, "You are in no fit state to leave this hospital, let alone thinking of discharging yourself, I strongly recommend you have second thoughts about that, it is more than possible that you will suffer from dizzy spells for some time, and your wound need a daily dressing change for a start, and that will not be till about ten a.m. when the day doctor makes his rounds with a nurse, so for whatever reason you have for leaving you are making a big mistake if that is your intention, please think twice about it, and ask the day doctor's opinion."

"I'll wait until the dressing is changed doctor, but I won't change my mind about discharging myself, but thank you again for your words of warning." Jack replied.

After the day doctor had examined the wound and the nurse had changed the dressing on his head, the doctor explained to Jack that the hospital would not be held responsible if complications set in as that may well happen, and reminded him also he would require daily dressings for at least a week, and made a point of stressing he must do no driving for at least a month.

But Jack was insistent, and said he would stay one more night and promised he would attend the out patients department daily for as long as necessary.

The Commander at New Scotland Yard accepted the news that jack wanted to return to work after taking a week off for what was described as 'medical reasons,' knowing that D.C.I. Desmond Dean was not at all happy being on the 2 a.m. case and would be happy to come off it as soon as possible, although Roger Osborn was quite happy to be re-united with Jack Farley again.

The Commander summoned Jack to his office and told him quite plainly that he had spoken to the consultant, who told him that if he did not think he was up to handling the pressure he should put him back on sick leave.

Jack replied in strong Farley fashion that if he felt he was not up to the job, he would have stayed in hospital and although he did not have the final say in the matter, he had Roger Osborn on hand and Don Grant also if the American was given permission to be part of his team during his stay in the U.K.

The Commander was thoughtful for a few minutes then agreed to the proposal, telling Jack that he would be back on duty a week from today, but any indication of a relapse and he would be off the case immediately!

D.C.I. Desmond Dean was pleased to be told of the new arrangements by the commander although not showing it, but inwardly he breathed a sigh of relief when told D.C.I. Farley would be taking over the 2 a.m. murder Case again, and that he would be given a different assignment.

He was just hoping no more incidences occurred during the coming week that he would be called on to attended too, or be in charge of, apart from checking out last night's Lambeth murder, although he was pleasantly surprised to find that for the next few days he would have the American Don Grant, as an 'observer' to assist in any way needed, and Roger Osborn who has been on the case from the start, so speech wise he knew he only had to make the odd umm and arrh and 'what do you think?'

And he would make notes of what he saw and what was said.

Roger Osborn had not met Don Grant before, and was intrigued to hear how the N.Y.P.D. and the F.B.I. worked, also how he started out to be in the police force, so while they were in the canteen for their morning toast and coffee Don began his story. "I was born in New York and our family lived in the Bronx district, a tough, 'no-go' area unless you either had to go there for some reason or lived there, our family consisted of Mam, Pappa, Grandpappy, my two brothers and myself, Pappa was a construction worker, and worked all over New York as a crane driver on the skyscrapers, and as kids we were often in fights with other kids as we would not join their gangs to fight the coloured gangs in the area, we always said, 'No Way 'and at times used baseball bats, chunks of wood and anything lying around if any of them came at us, then we moved to a better area and I always wanted to be a cop. after high school, until I joined the New York Police Department, worked at it and took a written test to become an F.B.I. agent, in that role we can be moved all over the states as and when needed, also many times we are called to any state, small town or city that feel they need our help, and yes, we do carry guns, and use them when we have to, stateside people are used to sleeping with a gun under their pillow.

We are also able to arrest any wanted criminals in any state.

I met Jack and Nick in Miami and am over here on an exchange programme and staying for Nick's wedding next month, my job really doesn't allow me to get married, as I would never be in one place for very long, but it is the life I chose after seeing some old George Raft and

James Cagney movies, so I swotted hard and papa put me through high school and I love it."

Roger said. "I am happily married with two children and moved to London to better myself, it is very different to where I was, but like you Don, I love it.

At that moment Alex Ford came across and said, "Hi Fellows, can anyone join in?" "Sit down Alex," Roger said, " I suppose you've heard about the latest Lambeth embankment murder? we are waiting to get a buzz to go there, any minute now I think."

"Yes I have," Alex replied, "I was in the wrong place last night, I was patrolling Westminster and it was a shame as I would have given anything to have been able to stop him murdering another woman, anyway the hospital informs me that Jack will be out today, but you two will be his chaperones until he is well enough and back on his feet, but if you need a break or are called to another job I will swing it in the stores and take over till you get back, it will be like old times being with him again."

"O.k. Alex, we will bear in mind, "Nick said. "I think Jack would like that as well as it will make him remember the old days with you, and we want him fit for the wedding as he will be walking her down the aisle, so he must look his best."

"Nice one," said Alex, "Trust me; he will be in safe hands!"

Moments later the three men were instructed to make their way to Lambeth embankment, a response car is waiting outside to take them there now.

When the three men arrived at the Lambeth Embankment a small tent had been erected and the jovial police doctor came out removing his rubber gloves and smiling said. "Morning gents, here we go again, it's definitely the same killer, the small trademarks he leaves remain in most cases, like the length of the cut, or the depth, and even the shoulder marks when he uses pressure, I think it maybe someone most of them knew, or at least trusted as mostly there is no sign of a struggle, or at most until it is too late to

do anything about it, anyway lads, she is all yours now until she goes for an autopsy, tatty bye boys, see you later."
As he went off whistling a tune, D.C.I. Desmond Dean said. "He acts as if it's nothing more than just taking someone's pulse, and now I bet he goes off somewhere and has a big meal."
"Your right Desmond," Nick said, "I've known him for years and he's always been the same, but I guess we had better check out if she had any relations and why she may have been in this place at that particular time, it's possible she may have been on night cleaning work, but the way she is dressed I don't think so, sometimes I wonder why a woman on her own doesn't get a taxi cab either to where she is going, or back home where she lives,"
Then turning to D.C.I. Dean, asked him, "Do you minded me taking over?"
"Not at all old chap, go right ahead, I find it interesting to see how you handle things!" replied the D.C.I.
"Right," said Nick, "Roger mate, you will

do the job Jack Farley used to put on my plate, once we confirm the name and address of this unfortunate woman, it will be you who has the sad task of informing the husband or relatives of what happened, make sure it is in your report, Don if you will make a note of all the contents of her handbag, hopefully an address, we can start now."

"Got it all here Nick old buddy," Don said after a couple of minutes, "Her address, her name and her house keys are all here, her name is Judy Kent and she is a Lambeth woman, it would seem she had been to an old school reunion, as she has an invitation here for tonight from eight p.m. till 1 a.m. also a mobile phone that I will leave for you to check on."

Nick had a brief examination of the body before saying, "Very little signs of a struggle mates, either she was walking home with someone she knew who maybe our man or was walking home alone, as like a lot of people seem to think, 'That kind of thing always happens to someone else!"

Roger said. "O.k. Nick, I have her address, the response car will take me there now and I hope it goes off as it should, as this will be my first time having to call on anyone to tell them there has been a murder in the family." Nick looked at him and said, Roger mate, if you are to be Jack Farley's sergeant, you had better be prepared to be the one who gets those jobs to do, all the time I was with him it was always me! "

An ambulance pulled up shortly to remove the woman's body, D.C.I. Dean going with the ambulance, leaving two police officers at the scene until the morning was lighter and more examinations could be done.

Nick and Don retraced the way the woman would have come, as the school where the re-union was held was less than half a mile away, although the hall was empty and locked up when they got there. They knew it would mean interviewing all the former pupils of the school, and that would probably take days as it would mean about ninety ex-pupils to see, but if the three of them found out where they lived it would mean thirty each, but it meant talking to them after their days work was done, but if at least one saw anything out of the ordinary, it would have been worthwhile.

The following morning at 10 a.m. the three men were in the briefing room with the commissioner, Roger was the first to speak telling them all what happened. "When I knocked at the door I heard a man's voice say, "I know Judy, you forgot your keys and…" "On opening the door and seeing me standing there must have shook him ridged," he said, "Has Judy had an accident? Is she hurt? She is alright isn't she?"

I said to him, "You must be Mister Kent?, my name is sergeant Osborn, may I come in for a few minutes?" he said, "Of course you can," "Once inside I said, please sit down as I am afraid I have some very bad news for you, sadly, I have to tell you your wife has been killed, in fact we believe she has been murdered by the person known as the 2 a.m. killer,"

He shouted out ,"No it can't be, she only went to her school re-union, I took her there and offered to bring her home by car but she laughed and said, 'No, she might meet her old school boyfriend', she was really only joking saying that, as we have been married thirty five years and have four grown up sons.

It can't be my Judy, you must have made a mistake, she was really looking forward to meeting up with her old schoolmates again, and she even took some family photos to show around."

I replied, "I am so sorry Mister Kent, but would you please be able to identify the body tomorrow, bring someone with you by all means should you need too, a car will be available to take you there and bring you back, at twelve o'clock mid- day if that is alright with you?"

He replied, "Yes, I will be ready, I will bring one of my boys with me for support, thank you for letting me know so soon, I will see you tomorrow, good night sergeant."

Reporting back to Nick, Roger said,

"I can see why Jack made you do that type of work, but I did do it a few times in Berkhamsted, although it was never for murder!"

D.C.I. Dean was more than pleased that Nick Stone had taken over at the Embankment, but back at Scotland Yard he again assumed responsibility for the way it had gone.

Nick and Don looked just at each other and grinned.

Both of them knew that Jack would not be happy until he was back on the case, as he never liked to leave anything he was on unsolved, no matter how large or small.

Chapter 13

After a good sleep during the day with the help of an injection in his arm, Jack woke up the following morning at 6 a.m. feeling refreshed and ready to face the day; he swung his legs onto the floor and trying to stand up almost toppled over.

"Bloody yum-yum, that was close, maybe the doctor was right and I do need a few more days to get back in shape." he thought to himself, and blamed himself for not being alert enough to avoid getting hit on the head, then remembering what the surgeon had said, that if he had not moved his head to one side, the blow with the heavy weapon used would have killed him, so in that respect his reflexes had not let him down, but he knew he must have been followed and should have realised the killer knew him and it would seem he was on the killers list, although he was really just a shadow away if he could only remember.

He climbed back into his bed just as a nurse came into his one bed ward bringing him a bowl of hot water and some tooth paste saying, "Good morning Mister Farley, how do you feel this morning? you look better in yourself I am very pleased to say, freshen yourself up and I will bring you a nice hot cup of tea or coffee, if you prefer that, and a round of toast and marmalade, after you have taken your tablets of course, see you in about fifteen minutes."

"Thank you nurse, make it tea please." Giving him a big smile and a wave, she left the ward.

Jack cleaned himself as best he could, and sure enough, fifteen minutes later the nurse brought him in tea, toast and marmalade and his two tablets to take.

He enjoyed the snack the nurse had given him and had swallowed the tablets, then lay back drifting off to sleep.

But at the same time trying to go through his mind the people he knew that were over six feet tall, probably have a limp, and smoked cigars.

As sleep overtook him, he remembered his father's advice when he said, 'Don't let sympathy or friends cloud your judgment.' He first thought of Bert Hooper who could fit the bill well.

He loved to smoke Havana cigars and had a noticeable limp due to saving the life of young child who ran in the road as a car sped towards him, Bert had ran across and made a flying dive to push the small boy out of the way, but unfortunately his ankle was smashed under the car wheel and that finished his career as a cage fighter but even now he is a match for any man, his odds on being the killer thought Jack, 'No reason I can think of, only fifty to one.'

Next, Alex's ex-wife's husband perhaps, not yet questioned as to his whereabouts on the night of his wife's murder, or any of the other murders as yet, possible, at ten to one as he is well over six feet tall and has a slight limp so Alex informs me, and a known womaniser, and made a mental note to ask him to come in to help with their enquiries.

Next is Bill Hooper, as although he is very unpredictable, he surely could not plan the murders as the real killer does, and neither his brother Bert nor himself would have anything to gain by murdering anyone, but he is a cigar smoker! and has a habit of going out on his own fairly often, odds of fifty to one. He smiled to himself as he thought next that would be his very old friend and mentor Alex Ford, a candidate only in the fact that he was around six feet six inches tall and had a slight limp, but on the night of the Lambeth murder he was nowhere near Lambeth Embankment, he was patrolling Westminster all evening and got home around one thirty a.m. having been informed by e-mail from Nick Stone.

Also he had helped out on the Perez capture and other helpful tips he gets from his 'nark,' so the odds for Alex would be one hundred to one, and so far he thought we still have no clear 'favourite'.

Maybe Alex's ex-wife's husband could be just in the frame? for want of a better word he thought, as he smiled to himself before dropping off to sleep.

The telephone rang in the Coopers' mansion and on answering it Bert got quite a shock when he heard the other person say, "Is that you Bert?" "Yes it is," Replied Bert, "Your voice sounds vaguely familiar, and who is it?" "This is Johnny Chapman here," he replied, "Your old trainer 'no mercy,' can I call in to see you for a while? I'm a few minutes away by car if that's o.k. by you and Bill, I'm not trying to muscle in on my old patch, that's yours now, and I've been back in England some six weeks now getting the lie of the land again, I am holed up in Portsmouth as I am pretty sure the 'old bill' will pull me in on an old warrant for that gold bullion job a few years ago if they get the chance, so it's low key at the moment mate."

"Drive on in now Johnny," replied Bert, "Things have changed since the old days,

I'll tell the security guards on the gate to let you in, see you soon."

Some ten minutes later he was in the large lounge with Bill and Bert, sipping a large whiskey Bert had given him, and smoking a Havana cigar.

Johnny Chapman was his usual smiling self as he said, "Well lads the reason I am back is I've had enough of Spain, it's not my scene any longer," and gave a chuckle as he continued, "There are too many bloody English tourists over there! but the main reason is I guess I am homesick, and will take my chances over here, so I've been in touch with a few of my old team and have in mind leaning on the back of the ferry line to The Isle Of Wight, and taking it over. I can do it mates, the old magic is still there, it won't interfere with your set up at all here and being old friends from way back, I had to call in to see you."

Bert was the first to reply, "It's good to see you again john, so you want to get back in the business again, you can't be skint with all the wonga you made,

I know there was six of you on that job, three of them got nicked and were banged up, but yourself and two others got away with enough conkers to last until you would be at least two hundred and fifty years old! So why back to the old ways mate? and don't give me any old bullshit, tell me straight or not at all."

Bill Hooper spoke up and said, "If you tried to get back here I'd smash you myself."

Johnny Chapman stood up and looked Bill Hooper straight in the eye and said, "Bill, you'd have one hell of a fight on your hands, cos' I've stayed fit as old as I am, and your size doesn't mean a thing to me, you never scared me back in the old days and believe me you don't now, I didn't come here looking for trouble, but if it happens I'll meet it halfway, I came to see you both out of old friendship that's all."

Bert chipped in, "Easy you two, and simmer down Bill, all we want to know John, and we want the truth,...Are you connected in any way to the 2.a.m.

murders? Your size fits the bill, and you've been over here from the first one, if you are, we will give you fifteen minutes start then we will come looking for you till we find you."

"Cobblers Bert," said John, "I've got no reason to kill tarts or poncey M.P.s, you know that never was my line, anyway, you both fit the bill size wise, you with a limp and Bill could put a pebble in his shoe, I've seen that trick done before lads, you think about that, but I would bet my last penny it is nothing to do with either of you boys, and one thing I am very sure of, is both of you would top the geezer yourself if you had the chance, and so would I if the chance came along, one thing though boys, apart from the Ravenhill mob are there any more real villains to watch out for?"

Bert gave a short laugh and said, "There are a few gangs out there, some coloured and some white that have their own territories, they wear assorted bandanas for their own gang members, most of them are kids though and fight each other, but they would knife you in the back if you were on your own or you turned around, cowards mainly, there are a few of them that have guns but it's mainly knives now, but even when they are nicked the magistrates, Judges and the old bill give them laughable sentences or smack their wrists and tell them not to be naughty boys, if you do come across any Johnny mate, squash the little bastards straight away!"

John stood up to leave and gave a laugh, saying. "If you need a hand anytime lads, just call for "No Mercy" and I'll be here, so long old friends, areviderci."

Back at the hospital ward Jack took a few steps on rubbery legs to start with and then asked the nurse if it was o.k. to have a bath to ease his joints.

"Go ahead Mister Farley," said the nurse. "Just be careful and do not get the bandage on your head wet as that will mean changing it in case any complications set in."

Jack smiled and replied saying. "Thank you nurse, I shall be very, very careful.

"Stay there Mister Farley, I will run the bath for you," then grinned as she said, "Then the rest is up to you."

Jack spent the next three days resting as best he could with his laptop computer working overtime, going over and over every scrap of information available on the 2.a.m. killer, but could find no more than what was already on file, knowing that in the back of his mind was the answer he was looking for, and it bugged him, thinking that others may get killed because he could not remember a vital clue.

Chapter 14

Later that afternoon he had a visit from
his old friend Alex Ford who came in
smiling as he said, "Jack mate, you will
love this piece of info. It's from my nark,
and he's only just phoned and told me,
and as it's my day off I just had to come
and let you know, you remember that
train robbery heist of gold bullion a few
years ago? It run into millions, three of
them got caught and finished up in the
slammer but the other three got away,
it was always known unofficially that the
brains behind it all was John Chapman,
a former professional boxer and well
known villain who lived in Portsmouth
and went to Spain soon after the job
before he could be pulled in for
questioning, well mate, my nark is one
of the best around and is rarely wrong,
it's pretty certain that Chapman is now
back in England and is staying shacked
up somewhere in Portsmouth, and he did
have an address where you most

probably would find him, but you would definitely need assistance if he was to be taken in, as I can't see him going with you voluntarily.

But if the boss at the Yard agrees, it will give you a break from hunting down the 2.a.m. guy and get you back in the swing of things."

Jack laughed out loud and gave a big 'Whoopee,' saying, "Alex old friend, that cheers me up no end, and I will discharge myself as of now and head for Pompey, just hoping I get the Commissioner's approval."

"One more thing Jack," Alex said as he turned to leave. "I understand he has been back over here six weeks or so, around the time of the first 2.a.m. murders, and size wise he fits the bill, so be careful pal."

Jack shook his friends hand and said. "I will Alex, I will."

The doctor warned him to take things slowly if he insisted on discharging himself, and he must go to the out-patients department daily for a change of dressing and examination.

Which he agreed to do until given the all clear, and after that he only had to attend when notified by the consultant or suffered any head pains.

Back at New Scotland Yard he asked to see the Commissioner, who hearing the news about John Chapman, readily agreed, providing he took the American Don Grant along with him for observation and support, and informed the Portsmouth police who would be with you in attendance and armed in case John Chapman was armed with a gun himself. At the address with ten Portsmouth police officers, Jack Farley and Don Grant silently waited for Jack to give the word to storm the house, knowing that John Chapman would not be taken without a fight unless they were lucky to surprise him.

"Go now," Jack called out, and the armed police officers smashed the door down shouting police.

And four ran upstairs to search all the bedrooms and the other six looked in the down stairs rooms.

Johnny Chapman was in bed with a local slapper when he heard the front door being smashed open and guessed it was a raid looking for him.

Jumping out of bed naked, leaving the startled woman screaming, he knew he had no time to get dressed, so he stood by the door in his old fighting stance and as the first one rushed in the bedroom he threw a straight left and a following right hook with all his strength, sending the startled policeman crashing into the one behind him and they both toppled down the stairs falling on top of the two below them and onto their protective shields, giving Johnny Chapman time to struggle into a pair of trousers and go forward shouting, "Come up and get me then, the first one gets a busted nose!"

Jack Farley called out, "Come down now John, you know there's no way out, and you could get injured,"

The ex-boxer laughed out loud and said, "How many of you do you need to take me in, eight? ten maybe,?"

Jack called out again, "Come down John or you will be tasered, and that is painful to the eyes."

"Get stuffed," came the reply, "These stairs are only wide enough for one at a time, so try again matey!"

Don Grant spoke up and said, "Hey there John old buddy, I've got an idea, let's do it the American way, first I show you the 38.calibre gun Uncle Sam gave to me when I first became a law man, now I point it at you like now, and if you don't come down straight away I'm gonna blow you away, you have just five seconds to make your mind up before I pull the trigger buddy boy, and believe me I will, 'cos I get impatient when your guys just pussyfoot around, your five seconds start now!

The ex- boxer hesitated for a second then said. "Yank, you arse'ole, I believe you would shoot me!"

And he then started to slowly come down the stairs.

"Put your hands on top of your head Chapman, and do it now," said Jack Farley, " As my American friend thinks he is back in the States, and has an itchy trigger finger he would have shot you, so play it safe and no one gets hurt, apart from the officer you belted!"

Johnny Chapman just grinned and said. "If you would have knocked politely, I would have let you in, but tell me if you will, who squeaked on me?

I've kept out of sight for six weeks and not left pompey more than two or three times, and I know who it wouldn't be, so it's got to be someone I knew in the old days after a big reward or handout if I get sent down?"

"Times change," said Jack, "You were a big man and ruled the roost in the old days, you should have stayed in Spain or found a nice desert island with hoola-

hoola girls dancing round you, unless you missed the old faces and places and needed to come back, like as if it was a fix for you, no matter who you are or how you change your appearance, you can bet your boots someone will have sussed you out and squeaked to us as you put it, and I reckon you will go down for a very long stretch!"

John Chapman smiled as he said. "Tell the bit of crumpet upstairs to lock up as she leaves as I won't be back for tea!"

Chapter 15

Back at New Scotland Yard the commissioner was very pleased and said to Jack Farley, Don Grant and the rest of the team that came up from Portsmouth, "That's the kind of result we like, it's been a few years since the hoist but well worth the wait, nice going boys, you may think I live in an 'Ivory Tower' and miss a lot of what goes on between most of you, but you would be surprised of what comes back to me, but apart from that, I would say Alex Ford may well be partly responsible for John Chapman's capture, that man is an asset that helps us no end and I for one will be sorry when he does officially retire, that man has an outside chance of finding us the 2.a.m. killer! Don Grant and Jack Farley stay here the rest of you can go, and thank you all once again."

Jack gave a sly wink at Don and both looked at the commissioner intently as he said. "What the hell did you bring that gun out for? this is Portsmouth England, not The Bronx, New York or Chicago, America.

We have strict laws in this country regarding guns and who they are issued to, leave yours with me now, you should have handed it in to the armourer when you arrived here, and if you step out of line again, you're on the next plane back where you came from, do I make myself very clear to you?"

"You sure do Commissioner, I guess I acted automatically as I would have done Stateside, 'cos when you draw first you got the drop on them, and it worked in Portsmouth." answered Don.

"Rubbish" said the Commissioner, "The man wasn't armed with any weapon at all, and if you had shot him, as you said you would have, there would have been all hell to pay, give me your gun now, I will give you a receipt for it and it will be returned to you when you get on the plane back to America."

After the American had handed his gun to the commissioner, Jack Farley spoke up saying, "It was my responsibility sir; I did not tell Don Grant that here in the U.K. our firearm laws are totally different to theirs and I should have made sure his weapon was handed in on his arrival in this country, so if you have a reprimand to hand out it should be put on my record not Don Grant's."

The commissioner said. "Your record is not one I would show to recruits Detective Chief Inspector Farley, although your results are among the best, it's the way you get them that I often have to turn a blind eye too, just call this a verbal reprimand, now get out of here, both of you."

Back in the canteen the two detectives

had a plate of fish and chips, and large mugs of tea as Jack said, "The fish restaurant I go to is better than this, I've been going there for ages but they spoil me there Don,"

Don replied, "Your memory is out of tune old buddy, 'cos you took me there the other night, don't you remember?"

"Bloody hell mate I completely forgot about that, but now you reminded me, I do," said Jack, "I guess I'm still a bit woozy old mate but getter better I hope! My bonce doesn't ache as much as it did at first."

Don said, "It will take time, but it will get better. What do you think your ex-fighter Johnny Chapman will get if he goes down? Your laws are different to ours, and our penitentiaries are much stricter than yours, over here it seems you gotta call the inmates Mister, and they have menus' for their meals and games rooms and television, and then get day release!

hell man, at that rate they are better if inside, Stateside they are banged up twenty hours a day, and the food is take or leave it, the guards have guns and are not afraid to use them, and it's no different for the woman prisoners, they gotta wear the prison uniform, and it's no made to measure stuff, only the out and out villains and fools come back for seconds, but I guess you know that, and I think the rehabilitation programme is a load of old crap!"

Jack smiled and said, "I know mate, I wish our laws were the same as yours in some respects, but over here it gets easier and easier, I always think the punishment should fit the crime but there are too many do-gooders around and not enough prisons, but about John Chapman, well he will do a stretch, maybe twelve or fourteen years, but he will be out in half of that by our daft rulings, although I am sure he will be 'Top of the heap' in whatever nick he is sent to and will have other inmates running round for him, but in his day he was a good fighter and even now I think anyone with sense won't try to test him out, it will be interesting to see what happens when the other inmates find out who is joining them, especially with all that wonga, gold wise he has stashed away, everyone will wont to be his friend."

"Where is your old pal Alex?" said Don, "He always seems to know when you're in the canteen," "The stores is in the corner over there," replied Jack, "He can see the table we are on from the window by the door."

At that moment his stores assistant came over and said. "Alex asked me to watch out for you and to let you know he won't see you for a couple of days as he is laid up with the flu, and to tell you not to call in to see him in your condition as you may end up catching it and you have your

mate Nick Stone's wedding at the week-
end, so he will call you when his throat is
better, and he said a big, 'no visit' till
after the wedding!"

"Thank you constable," Jack said, "you
can go back to the stores now."

Then speaking to Don Grant he said,
"Damn it, I wanted to see him personally,
as I got a little bit worried about him
when he came to see me about John
Chapman in Portsmouth, between
ourselves Don, I am more than just a little
concerned, as when he spoke to me I
noticed the whites of both his eyes were
slightly yellow, it could be that is either
something he is taking for the flu,
possibly yellow jaundice or worse still,
coke or heroine, as at times he seems a
little on edge, but I've not noticed the
yellow before so I may be wrong, but I
must speak to him after the wedding, we
go back to far to let it go, and if anything
happened to him because I stood by and

done nothing I would blame myself for
not even trying to find out if, and maybe
why he is on drugs, I hope I am wrong
but I've seen it so many times before."
is in four days' time and you have got to
be on top form to take the lovely Candy
down the aisle, so forget about Alex for a
while, you know he would want that, and
if he was here now he would bend your
ear and tell you not to be such an old fool,
so it will keep till after the wedding and
don't you forget, you could be wrong!"
"O.k. Don, you are probably right, and as
we have the rest of the day to ourselves
shall I phone Sylvia and go there for a
free lunch? As she will be the Matron of
honour and Emma is chief bridesmaid."
"It sounds like bippy of an idea," laughed
Don, "Do it now."
Emma was at the garden gate waiting for
the two men as they arrived and Emma
gave them both a big hug and kiss and
then said, "Don, can you do a magic trick

now if you wanted to, or do you need
time to settle down?"
He smiled as he said, "Well now Emma,
sometimes I can do one straight away,
I have a bar of chocolate for you here.
And at a guess I think your favourite is
marzipan?"
"Yes it is," she cried, "How did you
know?"
Don winked at her and tapped his nose
as he said, "That's magic Emma."
Then he gave her a sealed up bar of
marzipan chocolate and said, "Break it
open it Emma." And when she did, inside
was an American ten dollar bill with a
picture of Emma printed in the middle of
it and the words, 'To Emma with love,
from Don."
She gave him a big hug and said. "That's
more than magic, it's a miracle!"
Then rushed in to show her mum what
Don had given her, followed by Jack and
Don. After a large casserole meal

followed by trifle, they settled down and talked how nice the wedding will be. Candy being taken by a horse drawn carriage with Jack to the church, and how many they expect to be there.

Sylvia suggested they visit The Richmond Theatre on the Little Green before they left for London to see the musical, "Oliver" which they all enjoyed and then took Sylvia and Emma home. Making sure the security was well established there before they left.

Chapter 16

At 2.40. a.m. Jack's phone kept ringing waking him up from a sound sleep, bleary eyed he picked the receiver up and said, "Farley here, who's calling?"

He became alert straight away as he heard the other person say. "Jack Farley? this is D.C.I. Desmond Dean, I know you're not back on this case till next Monday, but the killer has struck again, this time it's by the 0.2 and his throat has been slashed again, it's that Lib.Dem. M.P. Horace Holmes, the one that recently 'came out of the closet' and named his partner,

we have sent a car to keep an eye on his flat in case the killer gets there first and I have told him not to let anyone in at all unless it is a uniformed officer…"

Jack interrupted him saying, "Phone him again now and tell him to look through his spy-hole on the door if he has one, and that he must be shown an I.D. warrant card with a name on it, is that clear? do it now.

"Willco and out" came the reply.

Don Grant was in the room by this time and grasping what the conversation was about said to Jack, "It's not your call yet old buddy, you know that, your scene starts next monday so stay away till then and concentrate on your buddies wedding."

Jack was wide awake now and said, "Don, I know your right, and the Commissioner will chew me over if I put my two Penerth in now, but I feel responsible in a way, as I am sure I have the answer in the back of my mind who I should be saying 'you're nicked!' to, and the sooner the better Don."

Don looked at his friend and said, "Look here old buddy, we had a few arguments in Miami if you remember, and maybe I could have saved a few guys lives if I had handled things in a different way, but hey, we are only human and we all make mistakes, so don't blame yourself for things that go wrong, think back at all the good things you done in your life and check the balance, you will find that you are a winner!"

Jack smiled and said. "Thanks for that Don, I know you're right, on Monday I take over, till then it's D.C.I.Dean's case and he has sergeant Osborn with him, and that man is thorough and by the book, so let's go back to bed."

Twenty minutes later the phone rang again, this time Don Grant answered it and said, "Grant here, whose calling?"

"It's Desmond Dean here, put Jack on the line please, it's all gone pear shaped, the killer got to Horace Holmes partner first, and he has had his throat cut like the others before the police car got there, I would like Jack's advice."

Don spoke softly as he said, "Since you last call Jack's headache has got really painful, so I gave him a sleeping pill and he is out like a light now till the morning, but I understand that your Sergeant Roger Osborn is thorough, and is an experienced officer, I am sure he will do all he can for you, I will get Jack to give you a bell in the morning, till then, good luck."

Don looked at Jack and winked saying,

"That's his problem till Monday my friend, so don't even go there!"

"I know your right Don, and this time I will listen!" replied Jack. And promptly went back into a deep sleep.

On the day of the wedding, Jack and Don arrived early to make sure things ran smoothly, with nothing out of the ordinary until Nick got panicky saying, "It's ten o'clock Saturday morning and I can't find my cufflinks, I had them last night and now I can't find them."

"Simmer down Nick; you put them in your waistcoat for safe keeping, and remember you have about one hundred and fifty people in the church and at the reception, and it's a lovely sunny day so it will be a great day all round and I am very proud you chose me to walk your lovely bride Candy down the aisle."

"Who else but you Jack?" Nick replied, "Anyway Candy wouldn't have wanted anyone else but you, and I hope you have your speech ready leaving out you dirty jokes, your corny ones are o.k. but knowing you, you will still put them in!"

The bride looked lovely in the horse drawn carriage accompanied by Jack, with Sylvia as matron of honour and Emma as the chief bridesmaid.

And the local papers were on hand to cover the event.

At the reception Jack's speech had the crowd laughing most of the time, even Nick said he had never seen Jack in such a funny mood and his Tommy Cooper impressions were life like.

Roger Osborn was there with his wife and two children, along with many other policemen and women, and everyone there enjoyed the occasion, and the rest of the evening went off without a hitch.

The following morning the bride and groom was chauffeur driven to a Butlin's hotel for a two week honeymoon, care of Don Grant.

The following morning Jack said, "My head aches this morning Don, but only from the booze and food that was there, you sure can hold your drink yourself, and after what you put away I couldn't keep up with you mate, but I will be on

the ball tomorrow taking over from
Desmond Dean and glad to be back,
and he will be glad to be off the case.
My new partner Sergeant Roger Osborn
is a marksman on the firing range, and
very dependable, that makes me very
lucky."

Don answered, "Well Jack, I've only got
two more weeks in England, and I've
enjoyed every minute of it, I just hope we
can catch your killer before then,"

"That would be a result," Jack replied,
"If only I could…"

"Stop there old buddy. I know what you
are gonna say," said Don, "You will
remember before long, It will come back
to you out of the blue I am sure, so come
outta that lane!"

"Your right Don, it will." Jack replied.

That afternoon Jack had a call from Alex
Ford saying, "Hi Jack, Alex here, if you
can recognise my voice, I'm still laid up
with the flu and sore throat and have a job
to talk, I just wanted to ask how the
wedding went? and don't forget to
question my Judy's husband, I have a

feeling he could be our man, I know I'm only a store man but I will feel better one way or the other if you can prove that he's innocent or guilty."

"I promise I will do that tomorrow Alex, you just stay in the warm.

The wedding was a cracker, it went off wonderfully, it's a pity you could not make it but you look after yourself, and you're not just a store man, you was born to be a policeman and that's how everyone at the Yard classes you, so get back to bed and get well soon."

Don said, "Jack, you sure think a lot about that Alex guy, and it sure seems that he cares a lot about you."

"Well Don, between Alex and my dad, I learned so much, you can't put a price on that can you?"

Later that day they had a message from New Scotland Yard summoning both men to the Commissioner's office, and their boss was in an angry mood. "Sit down and listen," he said, "I've just had a long phone call from the prime minister. He says as we are the largest police force in the country, why are we dragging our heels over this serial killer?"

I explained we are following every lead and hopefully we will make an arrest in the near future, he again stated.

"Categorically all parties in the House of Commons and the House of Lords not only want this maniac caught quickly, but demand it! Horace Holmes was a well-respected and popular member of parliament and he will be sadly missed, I tell you know that if this person is not in remand by next Sunday at the latest, it will be handed over to another constabulary, and you will give them every detail you have on this case so far, also you will take orders from them, do I make myself clear?"

I told him, "I fully understand his concern and that we are doing everything in our power to catch the killer and should leave the on-going investigation in our hands."

His answer was, "You have until next Sunday Commissioner, the cabinet all agrees that is the best solution, good day to you."

Then he put the phone down.

The Commissioner looked at Jack and said, "Well Jack, you see what I'm up against from parliament, I believe they are more worried about themselves than the general public but whatever you need, if we have got it, or can get it, just say the word."

"Thank you sir, I have two interviews to do and will keep you informed." "Good luck Jack." He replied, as they left his office.

Hey old buddy, your boss man sure is worried over this case; let's hope we can crack it open before I leave for the States, who's the first one to interview?"

"John Chapman, is first," said Jack he has been back here in England long enough, but I really don't think he is our man, it is just not his way, but we can see his whereabouts on the nights in question.

In the interview room John Chapman just laughed at the two detectives when they asked for his whereabouts on the nights of each of the murders, "Mostly shacked up with a bit of crumpet boys," he said,

"I did visit the Hooper boys and took in the sights of London again, they will confirm that, not so happy with some of the changes though, but that is what they call progress. But look somewhere else for your killer boys, it's not me!"

After another twenty minutes they knew it was not him and he was taken back to his remand cell.

The next person to be interviewed was Alex's ex-wife's husband, Mike Moore. He sat across from the two detectives and said, "I know all the old rigmarole about you saying, 'this interview is being taped and all that rubbish,' just get it over and done with so I can just get out of here!"

Jack looked him straight in the eye and said, "Mister Moore, depending on your answers, you not just get out of here, as you put it, for starters where you were on the night your wife was murdered? you should remember the date and where it occurred! also proof of where you were the night the Member of Parliament and his partner were both killed by having their throats cut?

I notice you have a slight nick on your cheek, from shaving perhaps? Do you use a cutthroat razor yourself Mister Moore? "Yes I do," he replied, "But if you think you can pin those murders on me, you're very much mistaken, I aint saying no more too you guys till I get a brief here with me, so if you want to charge me, then go ahead and do it or let me go!" "No way my friend, we have twenty four hours to hold you for questioning and that is what we are going to do, we will provide you with a lawyer if that is your wish."

"Yes it bloody well is, and get one here now and not some idiot just out of law school!" shouted Mike Moore, "You lousy bastards are trying to stitch me up because I married one of your crowds ex-wife, she left him for me and we was having an affair for some time before that as he was always at work, she came after me matey, not the other way round and he couldn't face the fact she wanted loving, not listening to what he done at work all the time.So that's it till my brief gets here, I aint saying another word."

"O.k. Mike, it will be about half an hour before he gets here," said Jack, "Do you want us to get a search warrant for us to search your flat now, or will you wait till you are either out on bail or free to go?"

"Not till I'm there buster," he replied, "I'd not put it past you lot to plant something there and then 'find it' under a cushion, you wait till I'm there as well!"

After his lawyer arrived and they conferred for some twenty minutes, he was let out on bail, and agreed to let the two detectives search his flat without a warrant, provided they done it that evening as he had plans to visit a strip joint.

It proved to be a fruitless search all round, and a couple of old receipts they did find showed he had been at a legalised gambling joint and at a strip club, which practically eliminated him as a suspect.

"Now it's back to square one by the look of it,"said Don, "Somewhere along the line we have overlooked something special that will take us there, but I can't think what, let's sleep on it tonight Jack and start fresh in the morning."

"Fine by me he replied, "It will be good to have a decent night's kip, and wow… I've had a quick memory flash Don, something just came back to me, it's all to do with cracking knuckles, I almost saw a face, but in a split second it was gone, once I am thinking for real and concentrating we will nail him Don, of that I am sure."

He gave a little chuckle as he said.

"Or my name isn't Humpty Dumpty!"

Chapter 17

The following morning Jack had a phone
call from Ron Ravenhill who told him
that Bert Hooper and himself had paid a
visit to the estate where Blind Ted lived
and laughed as he said, "You know what
I mean, funny how a bit of persuasion
makes them remember a certain face aint
it Jack mate? that was a short time ago
and we plan on a visit to him tonight!"
" NO," shouted Jack down the phone,
"This is my hit, if you push in and you're
wrong I'll bust the pair of you for sure,
and I mean that!"
Ron just laughed and said. "As it's you
jack, we will give you two days only,
then we do him in for Blind Ted and the
others, I'll phone Bert now and tell him,
just two days Jack."
The he put the receiver down.
Jack then made a call to Sylvia, telling
her not to worry, as it would soon be over
and things would be back to normal, and
let her know he was feeling fine.
Roger Osborn as away for most of the

day to collect his award as a marksman and Don grant was put on observing draffic controllers for the day, so Jack saw Alex and asked him if he could help clear up a few things that bothered him.

"No problem mate, I will get a relief to man the stores for the day, be with you in twenty minutes."

"Glad you could make it Alex," said Jack, as they re-traced the scene of the first two murders.

"My memory is back again and it is all falling in to place, Alex my old friend, I want you to tell me the truth, when you came to see me in hospital, and you took your tinted glasses off to wipe your brow, I noticed the whites of your eyes were yellow, is it because you're taking cocaine, heroin or some other drug? And are the tinted glasses a scam to hide the fact? as you have been wearing them for three or four years now!"

Alex looked at him saying, "Yes Jack, I do take a little of the 'white stuff' now and then, it harms no one else so what does that matter?"

Later, Alex asked Jack how the interview with Mike Moore went, Jack replied that he had a fairly good alibi, but he was still in the frame. Alex said. "I still don't trust him, in the old days he would have had the book thrown at him!"

Walking on to Trafalgar Square Jack said, "This is where poor Molly Ryan had her throat cut, she was on the game through no fault of her own, and she was inoffensive and liked by the patrolling police who turned a blind eye and left her alone, why would someone want to kill her in that way?"

Alex shrugged his shoulders and said, "I don't know Jack, maybe it was because she was on the game, and he didn't like hookers or 'ginger beers'?"

What would he have against them Alex?" asked Jack, "Was he abused as a child? I don't think so, as it was a full grown man that done the murders, no one would wait years long for revenge, do you agree so far with that?"

"I think so," came the reply, "But the killer must have thought it over first and had his reasons."

Jack spoke again saying, "What reasons? Alex, and then why pick on members of parliament mate? to put us off the track perhaps, or maybe he doesn't like their life style, or it could be it's someone that likes to read about himself in the paper or on the television news, no Alex, I think he is a nut case and a coward, as it is mainly women and men he knew he could easily overpower or take by surprise, when I think of poor old blind Ted, a harmless wonderful old man who just loved a pint of beer and spend a pound or two in the betting shop, it leaves a lump in my throat as only a moron would kill him that way and just walk off!"

"Maybe Ted knew him and reckoned he would spill the beans too you, but I'm not sure about that." replied Alex.

"One thing I know for sure Alex," Jack said in reply, "is if the Hooper brothers or Ron Ravenhill's team find him before we do, he will be 'brown bread,' dead, and it won't be a quick killing," said Jack.

Alex looked at him and said. "You could be right about that Jack, but first you have to find him, we have been to most of the places he was at, even the club that drunk kid tried to get in and the bouncers stopped him and gave him the elbow, and no joy so far, he's more like the Scarlet Pimpernel, 'They seek him here, They seek him there,' but one day you may well get him!"

Jack said, "Hopefully I can put this case to bed real soon; my memory is back in more and more flashes mate, and soon I'll have the answer, but can you be available tomorrow to give me a hand?"

"Sure thing Jack boy, then for old time's sake how about us going to the Tower of London like we did when you was my star pupil? they were some good days."

"Sounds great to me Alex, to the Tower after we check a couple of things out." Jack said with a grin. "Hold on a minute, Don wants a quick word."

"Hi Alex, Don here, keep a close eye on him, he is not as with it as he thinks he is,

or just makes out to be, Roger Osborn will see you both later on this evening, till then old buddy, 'bye for now."
Making their way to Lambeth Embankment where the last woman was murdered, Jack said, "Alex, why would anyone want to cut the throat of an everyday housewife? she had an enjoyable evening and could not wait to get home and tell her husband about it, the killer must have a very twisted mind! maybe a lunatic asylum would be the place for him rather than prison, if it was America he would get the gas chamber, and I for one would press the button!"
Alex replied, "Maybe she was in the wrong place at the wrong time Jack, but who can tell how a man's mind works, he thinks he is in the right to do these things, and I would not judge him, but I happened to be in the wrong place that night in Westminster, and who can tell where the next one will be? I wish I knew!"
Making their way in the tower they stopped and looked in at the crown

jewels. Jack said, "I believe a man called Captain Blood tried to steal them once, but King Charles let him off with a pardon, he was lucky, but forgetting that, let's sit in that corner over there and go over things shall we?"

Alex gave him a sidelong glance then said. "That's o.k. by me Jack."

"The facts as we know them Alex, are these," Jack said, getting out his note book, "Our man is over six feet tall, smokes cigars or cheroots, he is elderly but powerful and he has a slight limp, he is probably right handed by the way the victims had their throats cut, and has a strong dislike for hookers and homosexuals, I would like to know why? He really enjoys what he is doing, and inflicting fear and pain gives him a feeling of power.

But mostly he has had inside knowledge as to information that the general public could not know about, nor could most of the police officers stationed at The Yard, so it had to be an insider that had access one way or another.

The renowned Danish Tarot reader known as Opal Lady, Carol Mortensen, reminded me of my rookie days when she said she had a phone call from who she believed was the murderer, and as he spoke she distinctly heard him crack his knuckles."

And shaking his head, Jack said, "Just like you are doing now Alex! and I recall you even done it when I introduced you to the American Don Grant of the F.B.I. Then you made a big thing saying you were in Westminster and not at Lambeth Embankment when that poor lady was killed, but you had no proof of that because that was just a ploy to cover your tracks, but tell me why Alex?

You were my tutor and taught me so much, and I really respected you and looked up to both you and my dad. I know you are the 2.a.m. killer, and it is with great sadness that I am placing you under arrest for a series of murders.

You know you rights so I won't repeat them to you now, but before I take you in, tell me the real reasons why!"

Alex said, "I was going to deny it all Jack, but I will tell you the reasons why, it all began with my wife Judy walking out on me, she said it was either her or the police force as I was away for days on end sometimes, and she wanted to start a family as much as I did, but not if I was not by her side all the time, and she again said I should get another job away from the police.

I said no way will I do that, and volunteered all the more, it was then she picked up with Mike Moore even though we were still married.

When I found out what was going on is when I slapped her hard around the face, she threw a few things in a suitcase and walked out of the door.

He was a womaniser and gambler, and before long he had her on the game mate, yes he did just that and thought nothing of it, and the money she got from clients he took off her and gambled it away.

That's what I've got against hookers, they can break up marriages and each time I see one I can see my Judy's face, and imagine some stinking drunk in bed with her, and why the 'ginger beers'? well, there are other so called police officers around that are as poofter as they come, and when they found out we had split up they made a meal of it at my expense, laughing and joking and telling me to be like them and making obscene gestures.

I came close to murder then Jack, but I took to the white stuff to calm me down, just a little at first,   then I guess I became addicted to it."

"Why didn't you confide in me or my dad Alex? we could have helped you in some way, or at least my dad would have," asked Jack.

Alex shook his head, and said, "You was the son I wanted or at least hoped for, but you would always say, 'I'll get dad to help me for an hour or two with my exam papers, he knows them all backwards,' I wanted you to ask me to give you a hand, but you never did! I would have jumped at the chance.

When your dad was knocked down and

killed by that hit and run driver you were already a qualified policeman with eyes on the C.I.D. branch, and you got to the sod that done it yourself, that I do know! So we were just friends like now,
If you're ready to go now, so am I."
Jack said, "O.k. Alex, I won't 'cuff you, just don't try to do a runner on me! but I will tell you this, I have a small, but very strong tape recorder on me and all of our conversation has recorded, and just in case you got the better of me while we were out I have left three statements at Scotland Yard of how and why I know you are guilty, the first one is with the Commissioner, and one with Roger Osborn and one with Don Grant, so you see you are stitched up for real, and the public can go about their normal business at last."
Alex sighed and said, "You win jack, let's shake on it and call it a day."
Holding out his hand, Jack went to shake it but inches away from his own he saw a syringe with a shiny needle attached, and realised it was probably a fast acting

poison, so he quickly made his hand into a fist and slammed it down on Alex's wrist causing him to drop the syringe, but at the same time Alex swung a punch and hit Jack on the side of the head knocking him to the ground and giving Alex the chance to sprint for the exit and make his escape.

As he ran out into the street he saw a taxi and hailed it down, jumping in he said to the cabbie. "The nearest underground station, hurry mate, I'm late already."

"O.k. mate Tower hill tube station it is." Replied the cabbie. And put his to his foot down.

Meanwhile Jack Farley had got to his feet and rushed out after him, seeing him get into a taxi and pull away, only to be stopped by the red traffic lights

He swore, and looked round for another cab, luckily one pulled over to him, and showing the driver his police warrant card shouted, "Driver, follow that cab, and don't stop at any red lights!"

"You got it guv," the cabbie answered, "Wait till I tell my old woman about this, she won't believe it!" and roared off in pursuit of the cab in front.

Looking round, Alex saw what was happening and said, "Move it man, move it!" "The lights are red man," said the cabbie, "Here we go mate, there changing now!"

"Faster," Alex shouted, "Go faster," "Keep yer bleedin' shirt on mate, we're almost there," Pulling up sharply at the underground station he said. "That'll be…" Alex pushed a ten pound note in his hand, then leaped out of the cab and ran down the steps to the trains, pushing and shoving other commuters out of the way as he went, then vaulted over the ticket barriers, and down the escalator's on to the platform, with Jack Farley some twenty yards behind him.

Alex looked round, and for the first time felt panicky, he saw the carriage doors were just closing and knew if he could just get in the carriage he would be safe for the time being and make his next move.

Taking a flying leap, he managed to get

one arm in up to his shoulder as the doors snapped shut and started to pull away. Screaming in agony, he tried to pull his arm out of the door, but was pulled along the platform at a faster rate, until he was smashed into the wall at the side of the tunnel and was killed instantly with blood everywhere.

Some of the commuters screamed and shouted to try to stop the train, but it was all too late to help him before the train eventually did stop. The emergency crew and the transport police arrived on the scene in no time.

The sergeant in charge of the transport police was Jack's old friend Sam, who had kept abreast of the case, and even he was very surprised at the killer's identity and wrote all the information in his note book to put in his report.

Jack thanked him, and took his leave to go back to New Scotland Yard and was summoned to the Commissioner's office, along with Don Grant and Roger Osborn to give his account of what had occurred. He said he blamed himself for not handcuffing Alex a the Tower Of London where he could have arrested him there and then, but Roger Osborn pointed out that had he attempted to do that, he would most likely been poisoned by Alex's syringe.

They all agreed that may well have happened.

And it was left to the Commissioner to make a statement to the press and television companies that the 2.a.m. killer was himself accidently killed whilst trying to evade capture.

But not until he had informed the Prime Minister who in turn would inform both the House of Commons and The House of Lords.

The following morning the national Papers stated, "The 2.a.m. killer was a former policeman working at Scotland Yard." and "The Throat Slasher killed at a tube station." Another said. "Hero police officer risk's his life apprehending the serial killer."

Even the 'Berkhamsted Gazette' had a photograph of Sergeant Roger Osborn on its front page.

The three officers were given the next two days off and went for a slap up meal, Roger with his wife Elsie and children, Jack with Sylvia and Emma and Don Grant with one of the women constables. The next day Roger went to his beloved Berko for a visit to see some of his old friends.

Nick and Candy were still on honeymoon and sent their congratulations on closing the case;

And Don Grant spent the rest of his stay in England with his woman constable friend.

Later that afternoon the Commissioner called Jack to his office and said.

"Listen Jack, "I may be in my 'ivory tower,' but I have my spies, and your head pains may need a little more rest, so you are off duty as of now for another week."

Then winked as he said, "Perhaps Sylvia could help by nursing you back to health if she has the time!"

Jack smiled as he said, "A good idea sir, May I use your phone?"
